PARADISE VALLEY

Sam Paterson and Bobby Campbell rode to Texas to purchase a herd of beeves and bring them back to the Campbell ranch at Paradise Valley. But the deal came to a quick and violent end in San Antonio. In an alleyway, Bobby met his death at the hands of cattle broker Raven Dermott, who'd set his crooked black heart on taking away the family's rich Colorado ranch. Sam should have known better than to let Bobby handle money on his own.

After giving the boy a decent burial, the big cowboy sets off for Abilene to warn Bobby's innocent sister Ruthie that Dermott is headed her way. She's the only thing between him and Paradise Valley. But in Abilene, Sam finds he's a step behind—Dermott has already conned the girl and they're on the way to the ranch. If Sam can get to Colorado first he'll make sure Dermott never makes it to Paradise . . .

PARADISE VALLEY

Jack Curtis

GUNSMOKE

This hardback edition 2005
by BBC Audiobooks Ltd
by arrangement with
Golden West Literary Agency

ISBN 1 4056 8050 4

British Library Cataloguing in Publication Data available.

Printed and bound in Great Britain by
Antony Rowe Ltd., Chippenham, Wiltshire

On that oppressively hot midsummer day in the savanna land a few miles outside San Antonio, a few feather-leaved trees clawed at the smoldering humid sky while the sun, standing directly overhead, seemed to be beating them down with rays of brass. The pair of horsemen idling in the scant shade of a granddaddy mesquite took shallow breaths and spoke quietly as they waited. Beyond them, three riders combed through a small herd of beeves bunched in a lowland where there were still a few bites of bunchgrass left from the drought.

Raven Dermott, a big fleshy man with a full black beard, glared out at the riders, trying not to show his feeling of desperation and disgust for the world that was ready to crash down upon him.

The kid has the money, he was thinking. You can close the deal and leave the ranchers holding the sack, or you can take the cash from the boy and leave him dead in a strange land. Which are the best odds?

Robbing half a dozen ornery Texas ranchers on their home ground was risky. They'd hang him slow but not easy.

The kid from Colorado wearing new boots and a store-bought outfit meant nothing to nobody, except maybe his sidekick, and he meant even less.

"Lots of grass in Colorado?" he asked to kill the time.

"Belly deep." Young Bob Campbell smiled and lifted his Stetson to wipe the sweat off his brow. His yellow hair had been freshly shorn in San Antonio and gleamed like new-minted gold. A band of white skin between his scalp and sun-blackened neck showed where the barber had scraped him down with a razor.

No one would have guessed that his mother was an Arapaho Indian, legally married to his pa. In his case the blond hair and fair skin had won out.

Boyish enthusiasm flashed in his bright smile as he remembered the home ranch.

"We call it Paradise Valley. Dad pioneered it even before the Shoshone moved north."

"Pretty big spread?" Raven Dermott murmured smoothly, looking off at the bunched beeves through a haze of heat waves.

"We have about ten miles along Paradise Creek. There's plenty of feed, and the mountains block off the worst of the blizzards."

"Your pa must be quite a man to poke out into the frontier away from everybody." Raven Dermott had no idea of where this small talk would lead, but he knew his days in Texas were numbered. He'd tried to stall and then shorted his last contract, and the discrepancy had been caught in Chicago by a nosy bookkeeper. As soon as they had it nailed down solid, a U.S. marshal would arrive with a warrant. It could be days. It could be hours.

Inside he was ready to bolt, run fast and gain some time, but his calculating mind told him he'd never get far without running money.

"You betcha!" Bob Campbell exclaimed proudly. "Dad was smart enough to get there firstest, and he's held it against outlaws, rustlers, the Feds, nesters, and the Kiowa."

"Still going strong?"

"He's some crippled up with rheumatism now, that's why he sent me and Sam down to buy the stockers."

"Big family?" Raven Dermott asked, his slightly bulging eyes beginning to glow like those of a panther stalking a young goat. A broad-shouldered man, Dermott sat as easily in the saddle as he did in the oak swivel chair in his brokerage office, and in spite of spending a good deal of time buying and selling Texas cattle, he was still as tough and hard as pegged-out rawhide.

One of the riders left the herd and turned his horse toward their mesquite.

"Just my sister Ruth. Ma died when I was seven and Ruth was nine. But she run off with some slicker Dad didn't care for. Got a mind of her own, you might say."

"Went west?" Raven tried to keep his tone conversational, but as the rider approached, he felt a desperate need for haste.

"No, they went down to Kansas. Man name of Elam Stark. Said he owned half of Abilene."

"So your old daddy is up on the ranch all alone."

"Pretty much, except he's got the cook and the regular hands to play checkers with of an evening." The boy smiled, thinking of his father.

It was a chance, nothing more. Maybe a bad bet, but better than the federal penitentiary.

3

"All there, Sam?" young Bob called to the approaching rider, a tall, weatherworn cowboy riding a strong steel-dust gelding.

"All there and good as promised, Bobby," Sam Paterson replied. "Soon as they're bunched with the rest of the herd we can head for home."

"Then let's get back to town and settle up," young Bob Campbell said cheerfully. "This boy's plumb homesick."

"I'd best help trail this bunch into the main gather," Sam Paterson worried. "Think you can handle the business?"

"I give Mr. Dermott the money and he gives me a bill of sale with the tally books. That's simple enough, Sam." Bobby laughed.

"The money's in the bank vault?" Sam asked, double-checking, wanting the youth to learn by experience but also wanting to be sure he didn't make a foolish mistake.

"Yes, I'll ask for it, pay the safekeeping charge, carry it on down to Mr. Dermott's office, and get it all signed, sealed, and delivered. That right, Mr. Dermott?"

"Make it easy on yourself, you're getting them dirt cheap," Raven Dermott said casually, as if it were small change hardly worth bothering about.

Sam's misgivings showed on his long, lantern-jawed face, and Bob Campbell laughed. "Oh, don't be such a worrywart, Sam, I can handle it!"

"I guess you got to start sometime," Sam said, blaming his unusual hesitation on the muggy weather.

"Might rain," Raven Dermott muttered, thinking why the hell didn't it rain two months ago when he needed it.

He'd bet twelve-dollar beef would go to twenty, but

4

there'd been no rain and the ranchers dumped every critter that could walk onto the market and brought the price down to eight dollars, as low as it had ever been, wiping out Dermott Beef Company, leaving only the outward appearance of a successful brokerage.

Trouble wasn't new to Raven Dermott. He'd come onto the border early on, gambling, rustling, gunfighting, until he'd seen the opportunity to become a respectable cattle broker, a go-between for the ranchers around San Antonio and for ranchers in the north clear to the Canadian line.

But now, he thought, I'm back to the border days where it's dog eat dog.

Leaving Sam to work the cattle into the main herd, Raven Dermott formed the scene in his mind as he and Bobby rode along together. He pictured the bank on the corner of Main Street, then the boardwalk passing down a block to his simple cubbyhole next to the telegraph office.

Somehow he had to get to the kid after he picked up the money yet before he brought it into the office, where some nosy idler would remember it later on.

In his mind, he saw the false-fronted mercantile, the ladies' wear, the harness shop, the little walkway to the alley, then the barbershop, the land-title office, Ed's Eatery, the Maverick Saloon, then his own office.

The kid would stop at the bank and pick up the money, come out, mount his horse, ride down the street, dismount, bring the money into the office, and everyone in town, especially old Eshelman, always looking out his front window, would know it.

Coming into town, Raven remembered the livery stable on the cross street from the bank.

"Let's put up our horses first," he suggested.

5

"Sure, we're not going to leave till morning," the boy agreed.

Leaving the horses with the liveryman, they walked up the boardwalk on Main Street to the front of the bank, where Raven said, "Go ahead and get the money. I'll meet you in the office."

"Be right there." Bob Campbell smiled and took the steps up to the bank's front door two at a time while Raven Dermott strolled on down the street.

Making a show of unlocking his front door, he went inside, grabbed the heavy Colt Dragoon from his desk, and ran out the rear door moving with amazing speed for his bulk, back to a walkway that was littered with broken boxes and discarded trash. Creeping along slowly so as not to be seen from the street, he came to a lopsided barrel stuffed with junk, and waited.

There was no one out in the heat of the day, and he congratulated himself on picking such a torrid hour.

He heard the familiar jingle of spurs, the knocking of new bulldogger bootheels on the boardwalk, and timing his move exactly, he rolled into the open, choking and clutching his throat just as the young man came into view.

"Help me!" he gasped.

"Hey! Mr. Dermott, what's the matter . . . ?"

The boy carrying his saddlebags over his shoulder hurried to the big man now rising to one knee.

"What's the trouble?"

The boy was confused and unsuspecting.

"Shall I get the doc . . . ?"

"No, give me a hand," Dermott whispered as if in great pain.

Bobby put his arms around the muscular torso and tried to help Dermott to his feet, and Dermott staggered back toward the alley away from the main street.

As they reached the alley, Dermott spun away from Bobby's helping hand, brought the heavy Dragoon from his waistband, and smashed it down on the back of Bobby's head.

The boy fell like a sack of wheat, sprawling in a strange, awry position, facedown.

Instantly, Dermott clubbed him again and again, until he felt the skull bones collapse.

Tossing some wooden crates over the body, he grabbed the saddlebags and moved swiftly to the back door of his office, went inside, locked the door, and hurried to his desk, where he could sit down and look like a solid citizen.

After catching his breath, he wiped the specks of blood off his boots, cached the saddlebags in a compartment under the wooden floor, lighted a long cigar, and stepped outside onto the boardwalk.

Making a show for nosy Marcus Eshelman, looking up toward the bank, then shaking his head with disgust, he locked the door and strolled next door to the Maverick Saloon.

Ordering whiskey, he waited until Marcus Eshelman, the mercantile proprietor, came in for his afternoon horn.

"How's your day?" Eshelman asked, tasting the whiskey.

"I'm not sure. A young man was supposed to close a deal with me on two thousand head of two-year-olds, but he didn't show up. I'm supposed to be in New Orleans day after tomorrow."

"That's the way with these modern kids," Eshelman said, downing the drink and grimacing. "They don't have no sense of responsibility."

7

As he hustled back to his store, Raven Dermott felt the last of the anxiety lift off his shoulders. He'd pulled it off.

He would leave at dusk for Abilene after spinning his yarn to a few more folks. The big dumb cowboy would be waiting out at the herd, waiting and waiting.

2

At daybreak Sam Paterson rode the big steel-dust down the main street of San Antonio. His sun-beaten face, burnished like an ancient piece of bronze, was haggard from waiting with the new herd.

He'd kept a good bright fire going all night, but Bobby hadn't returned, and the trail was broad enough that he could hardly have gotten lost.

With dread in his heart, Sam paced the gelding down the nearly empty street and dismounted at the cattle broker's office. With dark anger he rattled the door, but there was no answer.

Striding across the street to the Winchester Arms Hotel, he woke up the clerk who was sleeping on a cot behind the desk.

"Bobby Campbell? No, he's not here."

"What about Raven Dermott?"

"He keeps a room, but I think he's gone. Try two-oh-three."

Sam went up the stairs three at a time and rapped

9

on the door. Nothing stirred. He tried the door but it was locked.

He didn't exactly step back and bust his shoulder on the door, rather he just leaned heavily on the flimsy affair and felt the latch snap free and the door swing open.

The bed was rumpled and empty, the closet nearly bare. The bureau contained only castoffs, and there was no valise or carpetbag. Raven Dermott had left nothing of value to come back for.

Leaping down the stairs, Sam Paterson burst into the street trying to think of where to look next so early in the day.

The Maverick Saloon's doors were open and a little lamplight filtered through. Maybe the kid had been foolish enough to go drinking with some fast-talking thieves.

He found the bartender asleep on top of the bar, his feet bare and dirty.

Sam rapped him on the shoulder until he blinked and turned his head to look up into Sam's blazing eyes.

"No yellow-headed kid come in last night. I seen him once with you, but not since . . ."

Sam hurried out the batwing doors to Ed's Eatery, where a thin, hollow-eyed man and his dumpling of a wife with frizzy hair were opening up for the early breakfast trade. The woman was grinding coffee, and the man poked wood into a great iron stove on which a blue-enameled pot of water would heat.

"Sure I seen him before. He ate here with you twice, I remember. But not yesterday," the tall fire builder said, wanting to hide from trouble so early in the morning.

"He wasn't here last night either. I closed up at

nine," the frizzle-headed woman said, keeping the grinder turning.

"Try the sheriff. Maybe he's in jail." The tall man's Adam's apple bobbed nervously as Sam's eyes fired like blue lightning strikes.

"He couldn't just disappear," Sam muttered, and at a quick walk turned down a side street to the sheriff's office and jail.

The sheriff, a short, paunchy man with a gray, sweeping mustache, was just coming out of the back room, hitching up his pants and looking tired out already.

"He's not here. Jail's empty," he drawled, eyeing Sam suspiciously, as he did all men. "Why are you huntin' him? What's he done?"

"He hasn't done anything, Sheriff." Sam Paterson tried to keep his voice low and even, but it wasn't easy, because the dread was like a cold snake entering his heart. "He's disappeared."

"Boys will be boys. Have you checked at Aunt Fanny's sporting house?"

"Not yet, but it's my last chance."

"If he's not there, come on back and give me a rundown. I'll be over at Ed's having breakfast."

Sam hurried off down the street and across the tracks to the next corner, where a two-story squared-off house stood by itself. In back was a place to hitch your horse, but there were only a couple of ribby mustangs standing patiently and a buggy with a matched team still in harness.

It passed through Sam's mind that this would be a logical place for Raven Dermott to spend the night. He had all the earmarks of a fast-living big spender.

He pounded on the back door until a tall, wizened black lady in a kimona opened up.

11

"Ain't nobody here."

"The hell!" Sam nearly ran over her as he charged on by into the parlor, which was decorated with red-flocked paper on the walls and imitation-marble nymphs cavorting about on wooden stands.

Going to the stairway, Sam roared, "Bobby! You up there!"

He took the stairs two at a time and came face to face with an older lady with sagging flesh and a wig of orange hair built up into a tower of braids.

"Hold it, cowboy," she said, holding a .45 caliber one-shot derringer on his breastbone. "Turn around and git."

"I'm looking for a yeller-haired kid, bald-faced but just about growed up."

"Not here," she answered in a low voice. "Never was."

"How about Raven Dermott?"

"Try the hotel."

"He's gone."

"The sonofabitch. He owes me a hundred dollars," the madam said, lowering the pistol. "Sorry I can't help. Want me to wake up a girl for you?"

"I've got business," Sam said. He turned and fled out the front door, across the tracks, and up Main Street again, where he found the sheriff cradling a thick china mug of coffee in both hands.

"Not there? All right, what's the big goddamned hurry, you can't let a man have a cup of coffee before he has to look another day in the face?"

"The boy was to pay Raven Dermott sixteen thousand dollars for a herd of two-year-old steers we gathered from about six ranches hereabouts."

"Where was the money?"

"It was in his saddlebags that was in the bank's vault for safekeeping."

"Did he get the money out of the bank?"

"Bank's not open yet."

"All right, give me a minute to swallow this tar, and we'll roust out B. G. Hall. You might as well join me."

When the frizzy-haired woman put one of the big mugs of steaming coffee and a saucer in front of him, Sam poured some in the saucer, and lifting it in both hands, blew on it, then swallowed it down.

"That's welcome," he said, steadying down. By now Bobby was either beyond help or would last another five minutes. He couldn't be helped by Sam's running around like a rooster with his head wrung off.

"Where you from?" the sheriff asked.

"Colorado way. Heard there was good prices for young beef down here."

"You were right there. Ranchers'll give 'em to you if you'll promise 'em a good home."

"Them cattle aren't goin' nowhere less'n I see the bill of sale and tally books first," Sam Paterson muttered grimly. "Bobby's supposed to have them all set and signed."

"All right," the sheriff said heavily, "let's go wake up B. G. Hall. Nothing I like better'n disturbin' the banker at seven o'clock in the morning."

They rode the three blocks up a side street to a small mansion with a large front porch built of planed lumber and painted white, easily the most elegant house in town.

The two men left their horses at the gate and went up to the porch, where the sheriff banged on a big brass door knocker made to look like the face of a lion.

Nothing happened, but after the second time, an old Negro with pants on under his nightshirt opened the door and squinted into the daylight.

"He ain't up yet, suh."

"Get him up. Right now!" the sheriff said.

The Negro closed the door and they waited another minute until the door opened again, this time revealing a fat man, fully dressed but with his hair mussed and a stubble of gray on his unwashed face.

"What's the problem, Sheriff?"

"Simple. Boy disappeared. Yeller-haired, about nineteen, name of . . ."

"Bobby Campbell . . ." Sam put in, studying the banker's lidded eyes.

"Yes. He was in yesterday afternoon just before we closed. I personally returned his sealed saddlebags to him, and he paid me and signed a receipt for same."

"You have the receipt?" Sam asked.

"Of course." The banker flushed angrily. "I'll show it to you during business hours. Anything else?"

The sheriff glanced up at Sam and muttered, "Reckon not. Much obliged B. G."

The door closed again and Sam said, "Somebody got at him."

"Who?"

"Whoever knew he had the money on him."

They walked to the wrought-iron gate and passed outside to their horses.

"Who knew?" the sheriff asked.

"The banker and Raven Dermott," Sam said heavily. "And Dermott's skipped."

"Not necessarily. Dermott's always off traveling, buying and selling. He'll be back. Besides, there could have been somebody else in the bank, maybe a clerk. Maybe the boy stopped and told somebody, wanted to brag about carrying so much gold."

"Bobby wasn't that way."

Sam suddenly realized he was saying "was" instead of "is" and he slammed his fist into his left hand. "Goddamnit, I've got to find him quick."

"I can't help you no more without something to go

14

on," the sheriff said, his face closed as a bunged barrel. "You can find me in Ed's Eatery or in the office, if you uncover some real information."

The sheriff stopped his horse in front of the café, and Sam continued on, saying nothing. A terrible weight on his shoulders increased in pressure with every passing minute. A slow, silent sorrow sent its roots into his breast as if to steal his breath away.

One place he hadn't looked was inside Raven Dermott's office. He knew the sheriff wouldn't let him break in because he expected Dermott to come back, but Sam knew in his guts Dermott was moving farther away with every passing hour.

With the street still nearly deserted, Sam tied his steel-dust to the rail just down from Dermott's office and strolled back to the front door. This one was made of heavy lumber painted black, and the lock was solid brass.

Big as Sam Paterson was and heavy in the shoulders, it would still take him half an hour to break that door down.

Mounting his horse again, he rode to the end of the street, counting doorways as he went. Then, turning at the corner, he entered the alley and counted back to the broker's back door.

A cheap piece of pine paneling crunched under his shoulder and fell apart as he went on through into the small office.

There was the swivel chair, the rolltop desk, a pair of straight-backed chairs, and a file cabinet. Nothing else.

The file cabinet was full of advertising and old *Harper's Monthlys.*

The desk was locked, but it opened under Sam's powerful hands. Still nothing. A few documents of past deals, printed business forms and contracts ready to be filled in, a bottle of whiskey and a half a box of cigars. None of the letters indicated that Raven Dermott had a home to go to, or that he was even using his right name.

Sam felt as if he were being tangled up in long skeins of soft taffy.

But he knew he couldn't afford to be swamped under so easily. Sorting through the contents of the wastebasket, he found a crumpled envelope with some doodling on the back in pencil.

800 2yr. ⊐⊏

That was the Double Mill Iron branded herd they'd bought yesterday, Sam realized.

"Paradise"
"Ruth"
"Abilene"
"Elam Stark"

Suddenly he heard the front door rattle. He drew his Remington .44 and turned to face the door.

"Anybody in there?" the sheriff's voice called. "Dermott? Open up."

Again the door rattled, and then there was a long silence as Sam Paterson held his breath and waited until he was sure the sheriff had gone.

Then, taking one long, slow step at a time, he made his way out the back door to the steel-dust, mounted, and considered his choices.

The boy was kidnapped or killed.

The boy and Raven Dermott were both killed or kidnapped.

The boy was killed and Dermott was on the run.

The latter, although the most painful to accept, still made the most sense.

Walking the horse down the alley, he was so preoccupied he almost didn't notice the mangy old redbone hound nosing among the trash, almost missed seeing him tug on something, tumbling the crates and rubbish away as he hunched down and pulled at a new boot, a boot with flared eagle wings stitched into the uppers, a boot Sam recognized as well as the new striped riding pants that went along with it.

It took almost everything he had as well as what Bobby's pony sold for to bury him decent, and now, with the sheriff and the preacher gone, Sam Paterson was left alone on the low hill dotted with wooden crosses and a few marble tablets each seeming to be at a different angle.

A friendly breeze eased off the heat of the day, and Sam stood bareheaded and dry-eyed by the new grave.

"I reckon there ain't much to say when the luck goes bad, Bobby, except when I get to Abilene that sonofabitch will die a hundred times harder'n you did."

3

On the south fork of the Canadian River in northern Texas not far from Fort Worth, a tall, cadaverous young man with craggy features and long flaxen hair leaned over to inspect a half-grown tomato plant. He wore indigo bib overalls, a hickory shirt, and a wide-brimmed straw hat usually favored by Mexicans. His slender hand held a wooden-handled hoe.

What he saw on the tomato plant was indeed interesting, a rather beautiful creature, in a way, if you cared about such things, which he did, but above and beyond the soft, slick skin striped with green and golden rays was the munching maw of a mouth as it and its numerous kin worked at devouring the plant.

The tall gardener shook the plant gently and a few of the smaller worms fell to the ground, where he mashed them with his boot, but the sturdier ones continued to eat voraciously, and there was nothing for it but to pick off each one and drop it into a jar half full of coal oil, a chore extremely distasteful to him.

Hoping the plant was saved, he moved on to the next one, which was already half shredded.

A rattlesnake buzzed fourteen rattles near the next plant, and he shooed the huge rattlesnake off out of harm's way.

"There you go, Lord Byron. Be a good fellow, and don't come back. 'Lions make leopards tame, yea, but not change their spots' . . ."

He stopped to survey the truck garden he'd labored on for half the summer. It covered a full acre. He'd spaded the whole thing by hand in early spring and planted the carefully preserved seeds he'd brought from the East and from England in rows in such a way that he could water them with a bucket later on.

The weeds had nearly beaten him first off. Chickweed, thistle, murdock, dandelion, crabgrass—it seemed an endless list of wild plants attacked the area, yet he'd hoed them all out, and even eaten some of the young ones, only to discover a large family of gophers had moved in for the unusual feast.

Compromising with his conscience and giving up on Lord Byron, the big rattlesnake, for help, he'd bought strychnine at the mercantile in town, made tasty dough balls laced with the poison, and poked them down into the underground runways until that problem was eliminated.

Then the grasshoppers took the young corn, and the beetles and soil maggots went after the cabbage and chard. Now he had hornworm and spit bugs, all crawling about, engorging his remaining plants.

He blamed the bad luck on its being his first year gardening. Naturally all the wild predators would attack and conquer the inbred, soft-natured, refined, and delicate vegetables he'd planted. Next year would be better, of course.

Gardeners are noted for their patience and calm demeanor, and the Englishman was no exception. He had a tiny monthly allowance from England, and he believed he could create his own food and shelter, as he preferred both of these necessities to be as simple as possible.

His concern at the moment was to rescue the tomato plants. Then he would examine the watermelons and squash and hope the beetles hadn't gotten to them first.

Admiring the big striped watermelons scattered about on the gray-green vines, he leaned on his hoe and thought how easy it was to make a small paradise.

"Lord, 'tis thy plenty-dropping hand
That soils my land, and giv'st me, for my bushel
   sown
Twice ten for one. . . .
The worts, the purslain, and the mess of
   watercress . . ."

His reverie in Herrick's old poem was broken by the pounding thud of hooves and hoarse breathing of horses as a dozen crazy-colored mustangs came dashing up from the river, mixing and swirling like bright autumn leaves blowing in a whirling wind, mindless, strong, and sharp-hooved.

Suddenly the band of pintos turned and raced around in a muddled circle, as if they had been designed to destroy his year's work. Watermelons splashed red soup into the air, and big Hubbard squashes split and went sailing as the bright-colored horses milled, then burst forth once again in a beeline for the river.

Down the bank they charged, until they saw the big

cowboy on the steel-dust with a lasso rope in his hand and a loop built and ready.

The big lead mare shied too late, and when she felt the rope around her neck, she immediately stopped and hung her head as if thoroughly ashamed of herself either for going on the rampage or for being caught, Sam Paterson would never know. He did know that after he slipped the rawhide hobbles on, the others would stay with her, including the stud.

He reckoned if he could just drive them into Fort Worth, he'd make enough off them to stake him for the rest of his trip north.

Then he noticed the granger standing in the middle of a small field with a hoe in his hand. All around him were the scattered shards of vegetables. Even the carrots and beets had been uprooted and stomped to flinderjigs.

"I say, are those your horses?" the tall, gangling man said in a distinctly British accent, nodding at the horse herd slowly moving over the prairie downriver.

"Kind of," Sam said, surveying the ruined garden.

"Kind of?"

"I sort of took 'em off the hands of some Comanche off west of here a day's ride," Sam said, angry at being delayed but also feeling guilty that he'd played some part in eliminating whatever there was growing here a few minutes before.

"It seems that however doubtful your title to them is, your horses have just destroyed my livelihood."

"Maybe you should have fenced in your truck garden," Sam said, dazed by the keen aplomb of the young gardener and his easy manner. Most grangers would have been hauling out an old two-bore fowling piece by now and yelling about property rights.

"There are corrals in this new land," the English-

21

man said, "but there are not fences, as you must know. You do owe me damages."

"Can't pay nothing until I sell the horses," Sam said tightly.

"I'd rather not bother with a note of obligation," the Englishman replied.

Sam stepped down from the steel-dust and measured the man.

He was an inch taller and forty pounds lighter.

"How come you're doing this out here to hell and gone?" Sam asked bluntly. "Truck's for women and Mexicans."

"First, may I present myself. Thomas Lamb, at your service."

The tall man in the straw hat extended his work-hardened, slim-boned hand.

"Sam Paterson."

He had a good strong handshake, Sam thought, and good, level eyes, but he couldn't figure that little mischievous smile that played around his mouth.

"I'll bring back some money," Sam said, "if you trust me."

"I trust you, of course."

"Then I'll just cut across the river and push the bunch on into town. Won't take more'n a couple hours."

With that Sam mounted the steel-dust and cut across toward the horses on the other side of the river.

"I say, wait!" Thomas Lamb cried out, but too late to stop Sam from galloping away.

Running after him, Thomas Lamb saw the big steel-dust come to the riverbank and set back to slide down on his heels when a muskrat den gave way under his off hind hoof, dropping him on his side. Sam kicked free from the saddle in an instant and was clear and cartwheeling as the big horse rolled over, banging his head once but suffering no major damage.

Sam landed off in the sandy shallows and thought he was lucky to have found such a featherbed instead of landing on a bunch of rocks.

As he stood up to wade back to the riverbank, he felt his boots sink into the soft wet sand, and before he realized he was in trouble, he was already knee-deep in ooze and could hardly lift his legs.

The more he tried to squirm forward, the deeper he went. It wasn't the water that was so bad, it was that fine-cut sand that seemed to want to swallow him down.

"Quicksand!" Thomas Lamb yelled, clambering down the bank.

Already Sam was waist deep in the stuff and several yards from solid ground.

"Don't move," Thomas advised, and commenced whacking away at the bear brush on the bank until he had a large mound piled at the edge of the quicksand.

By then, Sam felt the sand compressing his stomach.

Thomas Lamb extended the brush into the shallows, keeping a mound of it between himself and the sand, but a few feet from Sam there was no more brush left to carry his weight.

Sweat was coursing down Sam's face, and it took all of his willpower not to panic and thrash away in desperation.

"Take the end," Thomas said, lying flat on the brush and extending the hoe to Sam, who grasped the forged-iron head with both hands.

"Steady now. Just a slow pressure," Thomas Lamb said, keeping a tight grip on the hickory handle.

Sam put his shoulders to pulling himself up and felt

the change. At first it wasn't much, just staying even, but the pressure was upward not downward, and the less of his body in the quicksand, the less the pull, so that, without speaking, the two men battered the insidious enemy. Veins stood out on both their foreheads, and sweat ran like a river off their bodies, until Sam's boots finally popped free, and lying flat, he let Thomas drag him to the cushion of brush while he backed off to safe ground.

Both of them were so smeared with mud they laughed while Tom led the way to a safe place in the river where they could wash off.

"Reckon I owe you some extra, whatever my poor carcass is worth," Sam Paterson said, as he cleaned his six-gun and reloaded.

"It seems I'm in rather an odd spot." Thomas Lamb smiled. "Having neither garden, farm, nor horse to find another one."

"A horse is not so hard to come by," Sam said.

"Yes, well, Sam, frankly old boy, I'm rather fed up with this particular part of America."

"You mean you want to ride with me on up the trail?" Sam asked doubtfully.

"Actually, Sam, I'm not as incompetent as I look." Thomas laughed at Sam's blank expression.

"Well, you know how to fetch a man out of quicksand for sure," Sam said. "Pack up, while I get rid of them cayuses in town."

Mounting the steel-dust again, Sam went back to the regular river ford, crossed over, and caught up with his herd. The mare was quieted down now, and Sam took off the hobbles and let her lead the way down the trail to Fort Worth.

After dealing with the local horse trader, he managed to end up with a fat mare saddled and bridled and a packhorse he had some doubts about, as well as four hundred dollars in cash money, a sum very hard to extract from any horse trader anywhere anytime, as most of that breed prefer to be on the receiving end when it comes to hard cash.

With the two animals in tow, he returned to Thomas Lamb's camp and found him ready to go.

"I travel light," Thomas said as Sam threw a diamond hitch over the bedroll, the small pack of seeds, and the rootings packed in wet moss. Then, with the spade on one side of the pack and the hoe on the other, they crossed the river again and cut into the wide western trail that led through the Nations toward Abilene, as unlikely a pair as ever seen on that route.

Making camp the first evening by a small creek upstream from the main trail, Sam built a small fire inside three rocks of equal size, using mainly buffalo chips for fuel, which made a pungent smudge of smoke clearing the area of mosquitoes.

As Sam searched through his pack for a bag of jerky, Thomas went off on his own with his spade.

By the time Thomas returned, Sam had mixed up a mess of corn pone and was frying it in a skillet.

"Mind a vegetable?" Tom asked, bringing out a batch of weeds he'd washed in the creek. At the bottom of each clump of green were a few small brown tubers.

"Them's prairie turnips," Sam said warily.

"They're also called prairie apples," Thomas said, and set a small pot of water next to the fire. Separating the brown tubers from the plants, he tossed them into the pot and added a few herb leaves and some salt.

"I don't hold much with such truck," Sam said quietly. "'Course if a man is starving to death out on the prairie without a gun, he might stoop to eat pokeweed to stay alive maybe."

The fried johnnycakes were done and the bag of

25

jerked beef was set on a rock close by while Tom spooned out the prairie apples onto enameled tin plates.

"It won't hurt you to try," Tom said. "They're really quite tasty and nutritious."

"Passed through New Orleans once," Sam said. "Man wanted to give me a banana. I said, 'No, thank you, I don't want to feel a need for something I can't shoot.'"

Thomas Lamb chuckled politely, savoring the vegetables.

"With a little bacon grease, they'd taste even better," he said.

"I brought a side of sowbelly, but that's for breakfast," Sam said shortly. "Maybe we'll kill a deer or a stray steer tomorrow for fresh meat. I hope that don't make your nose turn up."

"Not at all. I prefer antelope liver above all else, but the deer are equally nourishing."

Sam kept his mouth shut. If it was anybody else but the man who'd saved his life, he'd go off and camp by himself.

He only wanted the one thing on his mind. Just to catch ahold of the neck of Raven Dermott, then squeeze until his pig eyes popped out of his head.

As for Thomas Lamb, he had lived alone long enough to enjoy solitude, a condition hard to find in the world since the Civil War. Not the condition of being stuck out on a lonely ranch for months on end where most men or women went crazy sooner or later, but being alone with his friends in the earth and the sky and the communal feeling between himself and all that surrounded him, sharpened by past experience and learning.

He had no fear of the prairie, nor Indians, wild cowboys, outlaws crazed with whiskey, or anything else, because he knew that the earth and the rest of the planets revolved about the sun, and not the other way. Knowing that was sufficient to humble any arrogance of breeding or culture that might have been in his spirit. The universe was simply too big for one individual to fear or hate or be the master.

He was curious as to why the big, obviously competent cowboy was traveling up the trail without a herd of cattle under his charge, but that was Sam's private business, and he'd wait until Sam felt some need to share his story.

Next day, they crossed the north fork of the Canadian and followed alongside the northern run of the Cimarron through the Nations.

The following day, Sam passed by two big deer before he spotted a dozen antelope feeding in the tall grass and nearly invisible a half mile away.

Slipping off his horse, he motioned for Thomas to hold, and taking his .45–70, he dropped to all fours in the grass and sneaked forward.

At two hundred yards, he quietly levered a cartridge into the chamber, and holding the rifle to his shoulder, ever so slowly rose so that only the top of his head cleared the grass, sighted quickly, and as the lower neck of the lead antelope fitted on top of the bead exactly in the notch, he squeezed the trigger.

The antelope almost jumped, but even as its weight went on its hind legs, all energy disappeared when the ball tore through the upper spinal column.

The rest of the herd scattered so fast, Sam saw only the white flapping tails for a second and then they were gone.

After gutting and skinning the animal, leaving the carcass to cool on an old tarp, Sam handed the liver over to Thomas.

"That suit you?"

"Perfect," Tom said. "You're indeed a master of the hunt."

"Made a lot of noise," Sam muttered. "We may get some company for that."

"Another bridge to cross," Thomas said, aware of the great prairie, an endless sea of grass cradled and rocked by the wind with nothing else in sight.

"It seems like there's no one within a thousand miles," Thomas said, entranced with the vision of the western frontier unbroken and untamed.

"We'll keep the horses close tonight," Sam said.

4

The embers of the fire dimmed and one by one died away until only the great wheeling stars overhead lighted the prairie. Thomas heard the picketed horses munching on the rich grass and in the distance the yip and babbling of coyotes, sometimes interspersed with the long ascending howl of one wolf to another. The little prairie owls came forth flying low, hooting, inviting the mice to dinner. The sky was like black velvet pinned with flashing diamonds in trailing patterns, and far to the east a great moon was on the rise.

How lovely, Thomas thought when Sam whispered, "I don't like that Comanche moon. You know how to use a gun?"

"I'd rather not," Thomas whispered back.

"Just as well." Sam slipped on his boots and his hat and belted on an extra six-gun. Carefully putting a couple of buffalo chips on the embers, he fanned them with his hat until the fire glowed again. Then, cradling his rifle, he murmured, "C'mon."

Thomas didn't question the command. Sam's voice, even though only a whisper, held enough iron in it to make the danger real enough.

Keeping low, Sam led the horses down into a small coulee where there was some brush and darkness to conceal them. "They're off to the west," Sam whispered.

"Who?"

"Comanche. Maybe a dozen of 'em. They marked our camp before sunset."

"Why should they harm us, Sam? We've done nothing to them."

"We've done plenty to them, and they like a fight."

"Two against twelve . . ." Thomas said. "I daresay we can handle them, but I would prefer to parley peacefully."

"I told you, they got a weakness for fighting and stealing horses. They think parleying is woman's work, and they ain't much wrong."

"Very well, Sam, what am I to do?"

"They'll come in from the west, likely down this coulee and the creek the other side of camp. You take the lower side of the horses and if you see something comin', shoot it with this." Sam passed over his spare revolver.

"I'm against killing," Thomas murmured quietly.

"I'm banking on you to protect my back."

"I can't promise," Thomas said doubtfully.

"Think of how you'll look without hair. When it comes to him or you, shoot at him."

Sam moved around the tethered horses to be on the upstream side of them, then disappeared in the brush and shadows.

Once again the night revealed the silent universe to sea captains, caravaneers, shepherds, and desert seers around the dark side of the world, naming the stars and constellations, uniting their spirits with them as all men do in the starry tranquillity, accepting and interpreting the message that all is measured, all is planned, all is perfectly in order.

Thomas held the big Colt .45 in both hands, hoping he wouldn't need to frighten anyone with it, when suddenly, from the creek beyond the camp where the fire still gave off a rosy glow, he saw a slim form emerge, slithering into the open, and a moment later he heard the huge boom of Sam's .45–70 just up the arroyo. Now came the yip-yip cries of Indians doing what they liked to do best.

They were professionals. Their yipping wasn't just to make noises to terrify their foes, it was information and commands being passed back and forth in high shrieks, a code unintelligible except to their units.

Then came Sam's thunderous forty-fours crashing out death in the night. The Indian near the fire kicked and fell back.

The yipping increased in intensity from the upper arroyo and the creek, but there were fewer voices.

Sam's guns were silent as he reloaded and called, "Watch it, Tom, they'll come around at you."

Thomas wasn't so much afraid of the Indians as he was concerned about what would be the best way to handle the engagement. Suppose he offered them the antelope to make peace. Suppose he gave them his gun to show that he came without greed in his heart. Suppose he just gave them the gun and horses and said, go in peace my brothers. Suppose he whistled a lively tune, something like "Yankee Doodle," or something more sentimental like "Kathleen Mavourneen."

Suddenly before his eyes appeared a grinning face painted bright yellow and red with its torso painted white to mark the ribs and sternum.

31

Jack Curtis

He had never imagined such a demon from hell in his entire life, yet there it was glowing in the darkness, grinning with the joy of anticipation in owning such a fine flaxen scalp.

Leaping forward with a gut-shivering scream, a long knife in his right hand flashing, the apparition was such a shock to Thomas's nerves his muscles cramped, a spasm went through his body, and his finger pulled the trigger on nothing more than instinct.

A black disk appeared on the white-painted breastbone, and the Indian's scream cut off and piddled into a heavy grunt. Lurching backward, he fell against another buck with an arrow nocked and at the ready. The arrow flew, the heavy Colt blasted a gout of flame, and Thomas stood still, frozen, the Colt still held in both hands pointed to the front, despite the sudden ache in his shoulder and the burning sensation along his left ribs.

The Indians lay sprawled at his feet as he waited for whatever the stars meant to send. He would not move forward nor backward. He knew he was in the grasp of destiny, because he had achieved such a state of spiritual bliss that the brute instincts were removed from his mind.

Very well, let the stars decide, let the grand design move me, he thought, as he heard the hammering of Sam's Remingtons and the screaming of the dying.

He was slipping away but he didn't know it. There was the ache and the burn, yes, but there was the fading away into the darkness he didn't understand. He tried to tell himself to straighten up like a good soldier, but something else said it was time to take a nap. "Cheers," he said aloud, for no reason he could think of, and then he slid down on his side next to a pair of beaded moccasins.

Sam held his ground, although he moved from one patch of brush to another to confuse the Indians as to how many men were actually in the draw.

He'd tried to count, but they moved fast as cut cats in the shadows, and he was sure only of four hits. Even the brave lying by the campfire had been dragged away while others had attacked from the left so that he wasn't so sure anymore that he'd even killed that one. The battle had a dreamy sense to it, the Indians came in like phantoms and after a moment they disappeared.

He'd heard no Indians from the west for an hour and it had been longer than that since he'd heard the two shots from Thomas. He figured Thomas was dead, and accordingly, kept his back to the steel-dust, glad now that he'd worked so much with him.

Far to the west he heard what at first sounded like the slow rising howl of a wolf and then he knew it was the song of death, the release of feeling by a dying man as he respectfully and proudly implored his ancestors to make way for him, offering up his medicine, the amulet of his spirit which had been his vision, his other half, ever since he'd come to manhood.

It was more than a sad solo dirge, it was a cry that cleaved the moonlit heavens and made an opening for the changing soul to enter once again.

To Sam it meant only that the battle was over, the Indians had lost, and the survivors would go back to their camp wearing mud plastered on their faces and hair.

Taking no chances, he edged around the steel-dust and the big mare and packhorse on down the draw, where he found Thomas Lamb slumped against the bank.

In front of him on their backs, grotesque in the rictus of a shocking death, the two Indians lay like

33

lurid forms made of sand, only the paint on their bodies still appearing to possess life.

"Center punched 'em both, Thomas," Sam said approvingly, taking the six-gun gently from the clenched hands, "and you're still breathin'. I'd say that's pretty fair for a beginner."

As gently as possible, he lifted Thomas in his arms, carried him back to the camp, and laid him down on his blanket, even as dawn broke with a magenta streak cross the eastern horizon.

Unhooking the bib of the overalls and stripping off the blood-soaked hickory shirt, Sam checked the wounds.

Call it fifty-fifty, he thought morosely. The knife scrape along the ribs could have just as easily found the heart, or the arrow protruding from the left shoulder could just as well have penetrated the lung. Either way would have been fatal. As it was, Thomas had a fifty-fifty chance, mainly because he was young, healthy, and lucky.

Both wounds had quit bleeding of themselves, and Sam concentrated on getting the arrow out of the shoulder while Thomas was still unconscious.

The arrowhead had glanced off the collarbone and was still an inch or two from coming out the back.

Using his bowie knife, he cut the arrow shaft off about four inches from the shoulder, doing a neat and painless job of it. He then used his saddle and blanket to prop Thomas's body at such an angle that the back of his shoulder was exactly flush with the flat ground.

Eyeballing the trajectory of the arrow, he then lifted Thomas's shoulder and scooped out a small depression where he thought the flint arrowhead would emerge.

Laying him down again, he reached over for the iron skillet, and holding Thomas steady with his left hand, he raised up the skillet and struck downward, using the flat bottom as a hammer.

He hit hard, a sudden snapping blow, then held back as the flesh gave and the shaft disappeared.

Thomas groaned and his eyes fluttered, but the worst of it was over.

Sam lifted the shoulder, and gripping the blood-wet flint jerked the shaft on through the wound, then applied a bandage made from a spare bandanna.

Laying Thomas back, he built up the fire, put on a pot of coffee, and started slicing bacon into the iron fry pan with the bowie knife after he'd wiped it on his pants leg.

By the time Thomas was awake, Sam had finished breakfast, loaded the packs, and saddled the horses, and was scanning the west for any sign of another attack.

"How you feelin'?" he asked when he saw Thomas's eyes open and blink.

"Up the queen!" Thomas tried to smile. His face was dead white from the loss of blood and his movements were slow and tentative, but in a few minutes he was sitting up, sipping at a cup of broth Sam had made from the antelope.

"Soon as you're able, we're moving over to the river where there's some trees. We can rest up there."

"Those Indians I shot?" Thomas asked hesitantly, not sure what he remembered was real or not.

"I caved the bank down over 'em with the spade." Sam said.

"Is that all?" Thomas asked sadly.

"Well, I didn't scalp 'em, or cut off their ears, or butcher their privates, like they woulda done to you, but I'll dig 'em up and do it if that's what you want."

"Don't be mad Sam, it's just . . ."

"Kind of sudden, I know," Sam replied sympathetically, then helped Thomas to his feet and up on the mare.

An hour later, in a grove of black walnut trees on the Canadian River, Sam found good shelter, hidden and easily defended, where they could rest for as long as it took Thomas's wounds to heal. There was wood for fuel, and water close by.

With the jerked beef and antelope, they could hold out.

The only problem was Sam's sense of urgency to get on up to Abilene. He wasn't absolutely certain that Raven Dermott was headed there, but as he examined the back of the wrinkled envelope again, he could think of no other answer.

He must have gotten Bobby to talking. Talking about the ranch, then his pa, old Micah, then he'd mention Ruth with a smile because he always liked her no matter what she did, and then Elam Stark tolling her away with his stories about the outside world.

It had to be Abilene. Everybody figured that's where Stark took her. But why would Dermott be so interested? Why had he killed the boy? Damn it!

Dermott had a good enough reputation, and he must have been making a good living. Why would he throw it away for sixteen thousand dollars?

Why murder a boy in cold blood?

A sickness gripped Sam's midriff as he tried to work himself out of his tangled thoughts.

He hadn't even convinced the sheriff that Raven Dermott was guilty. Sheriff kept saying Dermott would be back in a week or so. Said Dermott had waited for Bobby until near dark, and then he had left.

But nobody went out on the trail at dark. If you was going traveling, you left in the morning.

It stank like a gut wagon. Dermott had made sure everybody knew he had an appointment he was late for, and then slipped away in the night. Probably only went a couple miles and slept out till daybreak, then hightailed it north.

Yet why?

No answer. It didn't fit any kind of ABC.

Had Sam Paterson only known it, a man dressed in tan pants and shirt wearing the badge of a U.S. marshal was talking to the sheriff of San Antonio at that moment. Frank Taylor had come down from Austin as soon as he'd received the telegraphed warrant.

Not a big man, but built like a barrelfull of horseshoes, Frank Taylor kept a poker face as he heard the sheriff tell his tale and defend his inaction.

"Everybody believed Raven Dermott would take first prize at a bull show, Marshal," the sheriff said carefully, knowing he'd made a mistake.

"Before he came here, he had a reputation that would puke a skunk," Frank Taylor said. "Where would he be likely to run?"

"God knows." The sheriff shrugged and tried to sound sympathetic. "He spent a lot of time in New Orleans and upriver. That's where I'd look."

"Maybe," the marshal responded coldly.

"You say he lost his whole roll betting on the price of beef?"

"It wasn't his. He was playing with other people's money."

"We was ready to elect him mayor, too." The sheriff shook his head disgustedly.

"Where did the cowboy go?"

"He didn't say. North, I suppose. He didn't have nothing left after the funeral."

"Mad, was he?"

"That was it. He said he'd take care of whoever

killed the kid, and I kept telling him, Dermott wouldn't do such a thing and he'd kill the wrong man."

"And neither one of you was right." Frank Taylor snorted.

"How do you mean, Marshal?" the sheriff said weakly.

"Whoever did it is going to get a fair trial if I can catch him before Sam Paterson does."

"I don't understand," the sheriff said.

"For all anybody knows, Sam Paterson killed the kid. You forgot to ask him where he'd been."

"Doggone it, I meant to." The paunchy sheriff shook his head again. "It just slipped my mind."

Raven Dermott had not gone north at first, he'd cut across due east to Baton Rouge, where he bought new clothes and gave himself a victory party.

He knew the riverboats, had once even made a fair living gambling on them, but gradually his reputation for dealing second and shooting first sent him on over to the border, where such things were accepted as normal.

By now no one recognized the prosperous gentleman with the long cheroot and a fine Panama hat.

Big, bulky, imperious, he stayed away from the gambling tables and strolled the deck of the sidewheeler appearing to be thinking about heavy decisions and momentous events.

Despite appearances, he was in reality observing every passenger with a cold intensity to make extra sure he had made it through with no one on his trail.

Compared to horseback traveling, the steamboat ate up the miles with deceptive speed.

Even if the boat swung away from Kansas, he was satisfied. Every day that passed the hue and cry over the kid would die, and every day that passed put him a little closer to his goal, and every day that passed he ate well, drank the finest spirits, and bought the best whore on the boat.

He had no complaints.

It might be the long way around to Abilene, but it was exactly what he wanted.

Strolling up and down the deck, he considered what a wild card he was reaching for and smiled to himself. He liked the long chances.

The girl might not even be in Abilene. Hell, she might be married to Wild Bill Hickock. That ten-mile-long Paradise Valley might be packed full of Arapaho warriors again. The old man might have died and left the ranch to a home for waifs and orphans.

What a joke, he thought, drawing on the cheroot and gazing at the muddy river as the paddles beat against the current. Along here the river was so wide you couldn't see anything much on shore, just the green and gray of the forest and maybe the outline of a white-painted landing.

Orphans, waifs, foundlings, brats! God knows he knew that story as well or better than any sentimental writer in *Harper's Monthly* who'd like you to think the little boys were being rescued from the streets instead of being enslaved behind granite walls and put on to piecework drudgery ostensibly to earn their keep. But it hadn't been that way.

He and his friends had no say about it. For twelve hours of working in a furniture factory they were given two meals, one of gruel in the morning and one of a potato stew in the afternoon. They slept in vermin-crawling blankets on a stone floor winter and summer, and the weaker ones faded away a day at a time until, one day, they didn't make the call to work. Then the mill wheel was stopped, the belts ceased slapping over the pulleys, the drills and lathes quit turning, and still standing at their silent machines, a preacher gave them a sermon about the virtue of working and the resulting reward of going to heaven.

He went in lost, alone, hungry, at the age of five, and he ran off when he was twelve, stronger and wiser.

It was his luck. Even at the worst, he'd always been able to escape, because he never waited for something good to happen.

So much for the Society for the Rescue of Orphans and Waifs. They'd taught him all he needed to know:

The top is better than the bottom.

In four days he arrived in St. Louis, but he didn't delay. He took the next boat over to Kansas City, and then found that he could board a train that would take him to Abilene, the end of the line.

From everything he'd heard about it, Abilene was his kind of town, Ruth Campbell Stark or not.

Thomas Lamb was feeling better. His wounds were healing without infection, and although his right arm was still in a sling, he could make do around camp.

> "Breathes there a man with soul so dead,
> Who never to himself has said,
> This is my own, my native land . . ."

Thomas Lamb quoted on the third morning.

"What do you call that?" Sam asked, poking at the fire.

"It's a poem by Sir Walter Scott."

"I'm not long on poems, I reckon."

"But you could learn."

"I wouldn't be against learning, but I'm one to start off on my right foot."

"Then how about a jolly limerick, Sam!" Thomas declared, radiating good humor.

"Shoot."

"There once was a lady from Wilts,
Who walked to Scotland on stilts,
When they said it was shocking
To show so much stocking,
She answered: Well, what about kilts?"

"Kilts?" Sam asked.

"It's what Scotchmen wear instead of pants." Thomas laughed.

"Well, I reckon I'll stay with rhymin' brands. Keeps 'em in a man's mind sometimes."

"Shoot."

"I'll show you," Sam said with a hint of a smile, and picking up a twig drew the brands in the soft dirt as he recited them with a simple cadence:

"A Spear 6, Rafter H, and a Diamond N

A Hashknife, Lazy X, and the Dice Seven,

There's Turkey Track, Buckle, and the O bar V

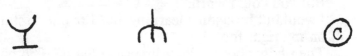

Take a Wineglass, a Pitchfork, and add the Circle
    C . . ."

"Oh, that's splendid." Thomas laughed.

Suddenly Sam swept the ground bare with his hand and stood up, his jaw set.

"What's wrong, Sam?"

"Circle C is Micah Campbell's brand. My boss's. It would have been Bobby's. I expect now it'll go to Ruth."

"Ruth?"

"Bobby's sister. Never mind. You ready to travel?"

"I'm sorry, Sam. I didn't know you were in a hurry," Thomas said, rising to his feet. "Of course I can ride. You know the English. Keep your pecker up and all that."

"Go slow a bit, Thomas," Sam said, regretting his short temper. The hatred and the need to purge it with the hardest vengeance he could think of was eating him up. He wasn't sure if even the riddance of Raven Dermott would cleanse his spirit and give him peace again, but it would sure as hell help.

Main thing was not to lose him. Catch him before he trapped Ruth in a web only the most rotten of human beings could think of. Stop him, hurt him a lot and long, then tell him why, then kill him.

Suddenly his mind switched as his jaws locked: What's got into you, Sam? You used to be just an easygoing cowboy, foreman of a pretty fair ranch up north, now look at you. Your friends'd be some surprised I reckon . . . Calm down. *Poco a poco,* one day at a time, *no le hace* . . . just . . . break out his eyes, nut him, and leave him in an alley.

Again the gorge of fury and grief rose in his throat and he shook his head and walked away because he was so sad he felt like crying.

"However bad it is, I'm with you, Sam," Thomas said quietly, putting his good arm around Sam's brawny shoulder.

Jack Curtis

"Vamos," Sam grated and went for the horses.

Next morning Thomas left off the sling and made his arm and shoulder work no matter the quick shooting pain. The gash along his ribs was now only a lurid scab and caused no problems, but the muscles in his shoulder took longer to heal. Still he reasoned, they'll heal better and quicker if they know where they connect and what to do.

"Don't overdo it," Sam warned.

"It can rest when I sleep. It can work when it's needed." Thomas laughed. "An idle muscle is the devil's workshop."

"My old mammy said something like that to me once," Sam said.

"Mammy?" Thomas asked with curiosity.

"She was black and shiny as a junebug." Sam smiled. "She smelled like lye soap, and I guess she weighed two-fifty. And my, what a smile she had."

"Was she a slave, Sam?" Thomas asked, a slight edge in his voice.

"Well, she'd been a slave until old Abe wrote a paper said she was free. 'Course her folks had been caught in Africa and sold in Charleston by the English blackbirders, so's the blame seems to lie on what folks think money's worth."

"I'm sorry, Sam, go on, I can be awfully stuffy at times."

"I dare say." Sam smiled. "So she was free to go and do whatever she wanted, but her home was with us and we was sharing what we had left after the war, like we had all along. My, I loved her a bunch," Sam said thoughtfully. "She was always threatening to whale my bottom, but she never did. And she was always sayin, 'You git to work on them books, Sammy, or you goin' to end up like us po' folks,' and I didn't and I have."

44

"You lived on a plantation?"

"Belle Yeux," Sam said. "Family was Scotch-Irish, but they put on the French airs, you know. Fancy traps and matched Hambletonians. Big lawns and smoked wild turkey on the table. There was a table brought from France that was inlaid with six different hardwoods, and twenty-four people could set at it."

Sam's voice seemed to change to a soft Southern dialect as he recalled his youth.

"Were you in the war, Sam?"

"Just a speck. I was too young. Only at the last, they needed what was left. Daddy and three of my brothers was already kilt. My last brother was on crutches with a raw stump of a leg. We was raised up to never quit."

"May I ask if that's what's bothering you now?" Thomas asked carefully, trying to avoid prying.

"No. That's past. I never quit. Lee and Beauregard quit. When they said go home, I went home, and looked at the ashes about a minute and a half, and then I just kept riding on west till I hit the Nueces River."

"That's in Texas."

"Yes, it is in Texas, Thomas." Sam smiled. "I met Micah Campbell first off, and hired on as a drover with him. Four months later we come into Paradise Valley, gave the Indians ten beeves, and settled down to work. That's the story."

"It couldn't be that easy," Thomas protested. "Didn't you fight the Indians and take their land?"

"You put things too simple, Thomas," Sam said grimly. "It wasn't like that. First off the Indians didn't like beef as much as buffalo. And there was a lot of land up there then, with a lot of buffaloes."

"You didn't murder them for the land?"

"No, we didn't. Maybe others did and are still at it, but Micah, he'd give an Indian a beef anytime he

thought the Indian needed it. Same with medicine or
flour or tools. Micah just treated them like neighbors.
Come a time, they'd come demanding, Micah would
explain that he would shoot anybody that took any
beeves without permission. Then if they went ahead
and stole one or a hundred, didn't make any differ-
ence, we'd all go out and shoot the dumb son-
ofabitches."

"Sounds like rough justice."

"Yes, I suppose it is, but at the same time, Micah
was trying to tell them the times were changing and
they had ought to be learning how to raise beef and
save their land. He'd hire on any young buck that
wanted to learn, and he married the prettiest Arapaho
in the tribe."

They talked on some more, and Sam even gave
Thomas the background about Bobby, Ruth, and
Raven Dermott. Now Thomas knew.

6

Ruth stepped from the small cabin, walked to the picket gate, stopped, considered a moment, then turned around and strode back inside.

She moved lithely, with a swiftness in her pace that seemed to fit her long bones and supple body, the way an antelope moves even in grazing.

Her hair was as black as her Arapaho mother's, more than black, because a deep-blue shine gleamed from the crow-wing waves that fell to her shoulders. Once her countenance had been happy and carefree, but today her long proud features with the slim blade of a nose and intense dark eyes were racked with anger.

In years she was a girl of seventeen, but the two months with Elam Stark had taught her a hard lesson. Her heels pounded the front porch as she went back inside.

Passing on into his back bedroom, she stood with her hands on her hips, eyeing the form of Elam Stark on the bed snoring.

A few months ago she'd thought he was pretty as a little spotted pig with eyes as soft as blackstrap poured on a tin plate, and she'd listened to his flannel mouth talk and thought she was so smart while he played her like a fiddle at a hoedown.

—O yes, he owned this, he'd done that, he was going on to bigger things, could be governor some day—

—My you're as pretty this morning as a little red heifer in a flowerbed. Ruth, you're just wasting your life away out here in the middle of nowhere with no one to admire you for what you really are . . .

—And she'd felt so good then, just full of sap and light on her feet as milkweed floss.

—'Course he never talked that way in front of Pa or Bobby. He made it look like it was secret talk just twixt ourselves . . .

—And then come to find out the sonofabitch didn't even want me. What he had in mind was putting me out in a sporting house.

—Maybe I was dumb, but he was a damned sight dumber.

They'd had a head start because Pa'd gone back into the breaks hunting strays for three days, and Elam Stark had darted in like a camp robber after a gingersnap, and she was dumb enough to run south with him to all his holdings in Abilene, as he'd called them.

Right off she knew she'd made a mistake, but she was too stubborn and proud to go back then.

What his holdings amounted to was this little rented cabin, and what money there was came from a sporting girl here in Abilene who had the loco idea he was her baby.

He'd bring home a big-time rancher and leave them

48

alone, with her not knowing the rancher had paid in advance for her favors. The rancher'd be expecting her to surrender like a willow in the wind, but it'd be a fight.

For not closing the deal and not marrying Stark, she'd been knocked around some, but that just backed her up all the more, and though she wasn't out bellerin' the news like a calf in a briar patch, she was still a virgin.

She'd been planning on moving out as soon as she could get a stake together, and toward that end she'd been helping Mrs. Eriksen in the bakery.

She'd hid her savings in a sugar bowl back in the cupboard week by week until she'd saved enough to buy herself a horse and saddle and enough left over to get her up the trail.

Then last night, when she'd been working in the bakery making today's bread, the scut had found her cache and played the fool all night on First Street.

He'd come in at daybreak, stripped down to his long johns, tried the locked door of her bedroom, went back to his own bed smelling of rotgut and his whore's perfume, and passed out.

She'd turned his pockets out, but he hadn't so much as a tin watch left.

A minute ago she was ready to just stampede out of pure disgust, but at the gate she'd thought better of it. A woman without money or family was fair game wherever she went. Any man she asked for a job would naturally expect a little something extra, and if he didn't get it, out you go, maybe to jail on a trumped-up charge, and there was no one to appeal to for help or justice, not even the other decent women.

—Girl, you sure used the brains of a grasshopper when you picked him.

What to do?

Snoring and farting, he slept, not like a little spotted pig on the bed, but more like a fat hog wallowing in the mud.

She rummaged through a broken bureau drawer and found a large towel, hefted it thoughtfully, then went to the kitchen and found a sharp butcher knife, which she slipped through the belt on her frock.

Next she soaked the towel in the water bucket, wrenched most of the water out, then, spinning it between her two hands, she formed a fearsome whip.

CRACK! The wet towel snapped on the back placket of his long johns. Elam Stark seemed to freeze, then elevate horizontally, his eyes opening in astonishment.

CRACK! She popped him again as hard as she could fire the towel.

"Hey! Hey, what the hell—"

CRACK!

"Ruth!" he screamed.

"Get out!" she gritted. "You're done here."

CRACK!

He was sitting up on the bed, cowering and protecting his face with his hands.

CRACK! She smacked him in the ribs.

"Out! I mean out! You git!"

"Wait! This is my house!"

"No more!"

"You're my woman!"

CRACK!

"Out, I said."

"Calm down—let me get dressed."

"Out, damn you!" she yelled, and whipped him across the face when he let his hands down to beg.

She commenced throwing his clothes out on the

front stoop, his boots, his pants, his shirt, his vest, and lastly his goddamned shiny derby hat.

"Out, you rotten bastard!"

"You half-breed bitch!"

He lunged at her, and she brought out the knife.

"This squaw's goin' to split you right down to your useless pizzle!" She advanced on him as he cowered back toward the bed. Her eyes gleamed, her smile said revenge, and she gripped the knife pointing upward.

"Wait, little sweetheart," Elam Stark moaned. "Don't be hasty. I'm sorry! Believe me, never again! I'm going to buy you diamonds, sweetheart, I'm goin' to do it."

"Diamonds big as horse buns, isn't that what you told me?"

"Honest, I'm due for a change of luck . . ."

CRACK! She snapped him with the towel in her left hand, forcing him to back toward the door.

"Please, sweetie, I told myself last night I'd turn over a new leaf. All we need is a little stake and we'll make it all the way to California . . ."

"And you want to sell my butt to make your stake, don'tcha, but I won't and you ain't."

CRACK!

Backing him out onto the front stoop, she slammed the door and dropped the bar on it.

"I'll bring the law on you, woman!" he yelled.

She laughed for the first time in months.

God, how good it felt to be free of the grub!

Now she could start thinking about making her way alone. Right this minute she could go nowhere, but she had her job with Mrs. Eriksen and that was enough security.

"I'll be back!" he yelled.

"You come pesterin' me again, I'll shoot you down like a yeller dog." she roared back at him.

"To see the world in a grain of sand,
And a heaven in a wild flower
Hold infinity in the palm of your hand,
And eternity in an hour."

Thomas Lamb recited with a broad smile on his long, thin face. "By jove, Sam, it's good to be alive on such a pure, fresh morning!"

"Sounds like you're all healed up and ready for another hog rassle," Sam said, his eyes always moving around the great pasture all the way to the flat horizon. An occasional meadowlark rose from its nest in the grass, or a jackrabbit would bounce up like a bomb under the horse's feet, while overhead the wild pigeons flew like scraps of shiny paper in a whirlwind. Above them sailed the buzzards, and above *them* soared the American eagles, pair by pair, rounding off a three-dimensional universe of life, big and small.

"Have you never thought of marrying and starting your own ranch?" Thomas asked as they rode along.

"Some."

"But you never found quite the right girl?"

"Found her easy, but I waited too long for her to grow up."

"How old was she?"

"Sixteen, goin' on a hundred."

"That's too bad, Sam. I suppose you can find another."

"Not likely. Two things I'm afeared of: a decent woman and bein' set afoot."

"Will she be back?"

"I reckon to find her first."

"That's a positive step in the right direction." Thomas smiled.

"She took off with a shyster feller to Abilene. I suppose she's married by now."

"I'm asking too many questions, Sam."

Sam nodded.

After five minutes of silent riding, Thomas asked quietly, "What was her name?"

"Ruth Campbell."

The pieces suddenly fitted together in Thomas's curious mind, and he remained silent for another ten minutes until he thought he could sum it up.

"The daughter of your boss and sister of your sidekick is in Abilene, and Raven Dermott may be on his way there."

Again Sam nodded without speaking.

"I can't make the connection."

"She's chuckleheaded as a prairie dog with the mumps. Maybe he means to kill her man, marry her, and take the Circle C."

"But her father is still alive," Thomas protested.

"Easy enough to put him down."

"You think Raven Dermott would figure all that out ahead of time?"

"Somehow he's pulled his picket pin. Now he's pure quill bad because he thinks ahead."

"Then you think he's north of us right now?"

"I'm hoping we can catch up." Sam lifted the steel-dust into an easy gallop, with Thomas staying alongside.

"Couldn't we telegraph her in Abilene?"

"I don't see no telegraph poles," Sam said.

"Then we've got to find more horses, so we can relay."

"I been lookin'."

Thomas realized then that Sam had thought everything he was thinking and a lot more.

"Take my horse, Sam. I can make do with the pack animal."

Jack Curtis

"I ain't about to set the man who saved my life afoot out here."

"I can do it, Sam," Thomas protested, just as they came over a low rise and saw three men crouched over a fresh-killed beef.

"Howdy, boys," Sam called and kneed the steel-dust to the left as if he meant to pass on by without stopping.

"Just a minute, stranger." One of the men raised an octagon-barreled rifle. "You too proud to pass the time of day?"

"No sir," Sam answered. "Not with a Winchester invite."

Coming close, Thomas saw that all three were still in their teens. They were also dressed in assorted ill-fitting clothes, dirty, and armed to the hilt. One of them, with a shock of dun-colored hair, even carried a cavalry saber.

Sam shifted his weight to the left, keeping his right hand resting casually on his thigh, about an inch from his Remington .44.

Thomas was reminded of all the predators in his garden, from the root maggots to the hornworms, so voracious and single-minded the ratty little crew appeared.

"Get down," the thin-breasted one with the saber said.

"I don't fancy that rifle on me as being sociable," Sam said, his eyes fixed on the scruffy wild-eyed kid with the .44–40.

"I want'a kill 'im," the boy said.

"Damnit, ease off, Monte!" the leader said, and the boy reluctantly lowered the rifle.

That's your first mistake, Sam thought, his face impassive. You'll never get another chance like that one.

54

"Looks like you found yourself a sidehill buffalo," Sam said, dismounting. "You need any help skinning him out?"

"No, we plan to just take the loin." the runty leader said.

At first Thomas thought from their speech they were from New England, and judging by their undersized bodies, they'd been stunted by lack of proper food.

"What are you looking at, highpockets?" the third one snarled, his hand on a pistol that seemed to dwarf his waist. Around the crown of his oversized Stetson were two fancy lady's garters.

"Easy, son," Sam said.

"I ain't no freak!" the boy yelled. "I can whip you any time!"

"Excuse me," Thomas said, "I didn't realize I was staring."

"A bloody limey!" the one with the rifle crowed. "By God, clear out here we meet the toff of my dreams."

Suddenly Thomas realized that the accent was not New England, it was old England, overlaid by the laconic western drawl as if they'd practiced a new type of speech.

"Liverpool boys?" he asked quietly.

"Once," the thin-faced leader said. "Then indentured as cabin boys on the packet *Homer.*"

"Jumped ship?"

"In Philadelphia." The boy with the rotten teeth and the big rifle sneered. "We been livin off the fat o' the land ever since."

"We come out west to cowboy," the leader with the saber said meanly, "but the barstards only laughed at us and made us dance . . . for a while."

"There's a herd about two mile west of us," Sam said. "They'd likely use some help."

"We just left that bunch. Sort of picked up a stray cow on the way."

Sam was desperately trying to think of a way that everyone could go on about their business with no harm done, but he couldn't puzzle such a happy circumstance out. These ratty kids from the slums of Liverpool wanted everything they owned, their guns, horses, clothes, and eyeteeth. Sam wasn't so worried about that, what he was worried about was killing three crazy kids.

"Tell the truth and shame the devil, my pa always said," Sam tried. "I get the feeling you boys are taking things that don't belong to you and maybe some folks are getting hurt for it. That about right?"

"Mighty fine-looking steed," the lad with the saber said, moving to one side.

"All that heavy armament you're carrying around didn't exactly drop down from heaven," Sam continued.

"I say, let me look at your revolver," the third one, with the furtive eyes said, stepping forward, extending his hand. "It's the latest, isn't it?"

"Yes, it is," said Sam, stepping back and keeping the leader in view on his right as well as the lad with the long rifle on his far left. "Thomas, take the horses off over yonder for a bite of grass."

"Nobody moves, gents," the leader said, his hand clenched on the butt of a Colt .45.

"Boys, I reckon you've smelled the wrong hound's butt this time." Sam smiled.

"Reach for the sky," the crazy one with the rifle said, grandly putting the rifle to his shoulder and trying to aim at Sam, who was not standing still anymore.

Whirling like a dust devil, Sam moved to the left,

drawing their fire away from Thomas and the horses and palming his .44 as he turned.

There was no way he could take time to pick out a shoulder or a kneecap amongst those wizened, crazed boys. All three had commenced shooting, and every time Sam came around in his whirligig maneuver, he fired back.

First down went the boy with the saber who had hoisted his big Colt and was firing so close; a bullet took Sam's hat and sent it flying even as Sam sent a ball into the scrawny midsection. On his next turn, Sam fired at the boy with the furtive eyes and a two shot derringer, a clean shot right through the broken beak of his nose. On his third go around, Sam heard a whoosh of air go by his ear and the explosion of the heavy Winchester, then he drove his slug through the left breast of the fancy vest drooping over thin shoulders.

As suddenly as it had begun, the fight was over and the guns stilled. A vagrant breeze lifted the gray acrid gunsmoke and spread it downwind.

Thomas leaped forward to the bodies still twitching spasmodically.

"Good Lord," he moaned, "the bloody fools."

The leader with the feral eyes and ratty teeth coughed up some blood, moaned, and when Sam bent over him, said, "Blast your bleedin' eyes . . ." and then came a very loud death rattle from such a small corpse.

"Sam!" Thomas stared at him accusingly.

"Don't Sam me. How many innocent pilgrims you s'pose they killed for all their trappings?"

"But . . ."

"But nothing. They was a pestilence I never made, and I'm glad I finished it," Sam said, retrieving his hat.

"Now let's get to jerking that beef before some herd boss comes over the rise and wants to hang us."

"But the bodies!" Thomas cried out. "How can you think of butchering a cow, when you've just killed three boys?"

"I recollect they drawed first," Sam said dryly. "Get to butcherin'."

While Thomas cut out the loin and a couple of large chunks from the hindquarters and put them in a clean flour sack, Sam was busy taking blanket rolls off the three horses and throwing them near the grotesquely sprawled bodies.

Leaving their bridles on and letting off the cinches, he made running halters connecting the three big horses and led the end of the rope to dally on his own saddle horn.

"Poor lads," Thomas said, securing the sack of meat to the wooden McClellan pack saddle.

"Poor shots and practiced cutthroats," Sam said, mounting up. "Give them credit, they could pick a strong horse."

With patience he started off his string of horses, gradually easing them along into a slow gallop that the steel-dust could carry for miles.

"But the bodies!" Thomas yelled when Sam finally hauled up, dismounted, and lowered the stirrups on a big rangy black horse.

"The buzzards got to eat too," Sam said. "Change over, we're going."

In a half a minute they were on the slow gallop again until Sam felt the hoarse breathing of the black, then he changed again to a heavy-barreled sorrel hunter, leaving the lighter Thomas to return to his bay.

Tired, dirty, and caked with sweat salt, Sam halted them for the night at the crossing of the Cimarron.

"I'll build the fire," Thomas said, his crotch burning from saddle sores.

"Then I'll handle the cavvy," Sam said, and commenced improvising hobbles for the extra three horses.

When he returned, the fire, made in a firepit used many times by passing drovers, was reduced to a heaping bed of coals.

Sam sliced the beef into steaks, found some salt and bacon grease, and loaded up the iron fry pan.

"Long day," he said in the near darkness.

"You're hard."

"I figure in general nobody knows nothin' about the feelings of others."

"But we left them there without a burial, not even a prayer."

"How many women and children you suppose they put in their three-way hitch and hacked off their heads with that goddamned saber?"

"Sam . . ."

"Answer or rest your pipes."

"We don't know that they ever hurt anyone."

"Thomas Lamb," Sam muttered, "we're goin' to ride in six hours. Eat your meat."

"I'm raw in the butt, Sam."

"I got time on my mind. Time and a man I'm going to kill for fun."

Sam put the half-full skillet on a little platform hanging from a tree, which passing drovers had set up years before.

"We'll grab a handful of beef in the morning and eat on the way."

"Sam, you have to eat some vegetables. You need carbohydrates."

"I need blood," Sam said.

* * *

Far to the north, a man old beyond his years, apparently strong and fit, yet walking delicately as if to put any weight on his knees and hips would send a knife of pain through him, moved out into the night and looked at the Big Dipper wheeling slowly in the northern sky as if anchored to the polestar beyond its pointers.

"Damn it," he groaned.

Near the stone-and-log house he could hear the cold waters of Paradise Creek rolling and tumbling on down toward the Platte. The big rustic house was set on a bench close by the first rise of the Bow Mountains, overlooking a valley big enough to hold five thousand head of cattle or so if the weather got that bad in the winter.

He felt exhilarated breathing the clean fresh air tasting of pines and birches. Here he'd come and set his own flag. Here he'd said, 'This is mine and I will be your friend or enemy, whatever you want.'

Proving it had been more than easy when the traveling parson married him to Snow Bells, whom he loved as no other woman in his life.

He'd have married her even if it had made it harder to get along with the Shoshones and Arapahos.

Yonder she slept beneath the blue spruce, and he expected to lie beside her when the great Manitou put him there and took away his pain.

But it wasn't right yet. He had to hold off even if every day was a misery. You take their tonics, you swallow their powders, you even put their copper belts around your knees at night, but nothing helps.

Still you have to wait for Bobby to come back, maybe with a bride already seeded.

Surely he hadn't fought the pumas and the grizzly

and the Sioux just to see a syndicate of foreigners take over the beautiful Circle C. Or worse, let the government take it and steal away its beauty through the usual government corruption.

"Great Manitou," the man older than his years prayed to the starry heavens, "bring home my son and my daughter."

God, his bones hurt. He thought tomorrow he'd ride over to the hot spring and soak awhile.

Raven Dermott that night sat on the velvet-covered seat of the railway car dozing between dream and reality. He'd reach Abilene in the morning. He was shaved clean, his hair had been cut short, he wore a dark, conservative suit and tie. He would pass himself off as an attorney representing a large land corporation investigating the investment opportunities in Kansas.

He was cultivating a New York accent, clipping off his words and running them through his nose.

And he was dreaming about the girl, Ruth. A name that could mean anything. How old? Fat, skinny, short, tall, dark, or fair? Her brother had been fair-skinned with hair like gold, Raven remembered with a strange thrill, remembered beating on it with the big Dragoon until it went to mush underneath.

She must be young, but already tamed to obey and please in every way. Hell, he wouldn't kill her if she made a good woman for him.

Mustn't jump the gun, he murmured in his sleep, a vision of a beautiful girl with full breasts, a narrow waist, broad guitar-shaped hips, and a delectable nest lying before him. Ah, that was Paradise Valley.

Ten miles along a constant river, grass belly high

every year, the Indians tamed, the house built, everything ready for the new boss to move in.

The old man?

He laughed in his sleep, his lips puckering and making sounds like a terrier yipping along after a bunny rabbit.

7

After cleaning up the mess left from the fracas with Elam, Ruth looked about the tiny house and felt like dancing or flying like an eagle.

For the first time in two months, the dismal weight of her folly had lifted from her shoulders and she considered the future. From what Elam had told her, it would be terribly hard to live a straight and decent life alone, but that is what she meant to do. Ma Eriksen was getting along in years. It wouldn't be long before she'd want to sell the big ovens and the business that went with them.

It would be hard work for a while, but she was strong, and customers were already rising early and coming to the bakery for her hot fresh bread, which she varied from time to time from the regular two-pound sourdough loaf, to the long, thinner French-style with the crispy crust, to an occasional batch with cinnamon flavor topped with sugar. Already Ma Eriksen was spending more time in her rocker and less at the kneading board.

It was too soon to think of a man to marry. She could never hold her head up so long as Elam Stark was alive, and there was no sense making dreams or wishing she hadn't been stupid.

Yes, when the moon was big and yellow, she'd feel it fetch at her loins, and she'd feel weak and fidgety for a while, but she would have to control that. She couldn't afford to make another mistake.

Through her mind passed the vision of her father before she'd run off. He'd patted her on the head like a little girl, not realizing she was already grown and ready to change into a woman.

And she remembered the big, short-spoken Sam Paterson, who seemed to be always there whenever she needed help. If a feisty pony tossed her, he'd appear to pick her up and set her in the saddle again. If all the men, rough, tough, scarred, and rope-burned, who only thought about raising cattle and horses, forgot her birthday, Sam Paterson would straighten it out and see she had a cake with candles and the whole damned crew to sing the Happy Birthday song too.

What a good man he was, she thought a little sadly. Of course he was years older than her, so she'd never thought much about him as a human being. He was always more like an uncle to her and Bobby, always looking after both their hides after ma died.

Yet there he was in her vision, big and powerful enough to take down a bull, and yet always soft-spoken and clean as a working cowboy could be.

The other cowboys on the ranch would buy a set of clothes and wear 'em for six months until their pants would stand up in the corner and the shirt was layered with sweat crystals, then they'd get some money and throw away the old set and buy another, but with Sam, he kept several sets, and every Sunday morning he washed his clothes in a copper boiler with yellow lye soap, and he always smelled sweet as the spring wind coming down off the pine mountain.

Darn it, why hadn't she noticed him?

Surely he was a lonely man.

She'd heard somewhere that his family had lost everything, including their lives, in that awful war, and his sweetheart had not waited for him, that she'd married a Yankee major, something like that. The story wasn't clear, because Sam hadn't ever told it, and so it was just made up of little snippets from here and there and filled out with guesses, estimates, and projections.

Sam and Pa always got along well. Sam with his polite respect, even in the middle of a fight with Indians or heading off a stampede, it was always, "Yes, Mr. Campbell, No, Mr. Campbell. Mind if I try doing it this way?"

Deep down, in spite of the rough life, he would have been a southern gentleman if the cards had come up right for him.

You never heard him ever complain.

He might come in from a blizzard with his mustache frosted solid and he wouldn't say how hellish cold it was outside, he would say how nice and warm it was inside.

As her thoughts rose and drifted about, something seemed to change her way of looking at him. She felt a heat in her body and a tingle in her skin as she pictured him smiling down at her.

Oh, darn it! Too late girl, too late. You made your bed and now you must sleep with the rocks.

She clapped her hands together to break the reverie. No point in beating that old dead horse no more. Now you have a chance to make something of yourself by hard work and a happy smile. Maybe it's not what you'd imagined your life to be, but by hell, you can do the best you can with what you got, just the way dad had to do.

Smiling at herself and her imaginings, she made sure her gingham frock was clean and undamaged from the ruckus with Elam, and seeing that it was nearly one o'clock, took her handbag, went out and locked the door, then walked up the street to the bakery, which was in the middle of the block on Main Street.

The loafers lounging on benches along the way watched her with sly grins as she passed by, murmuring choice little diamonds of wit:

"She can park her boots under my bunk anytime."

"What a haunch!"

"I got the rake for her hay crop."

"Lordy, I'd eat a yard of gut for a whiff of that."

"Looks hot enough to wither a fence post."

"I'd leave my spurs off if she asked."

There was much clearing of throats and coughing, as if suddenly an epidemic of catarrh had infected the male population of Main Street.

She strode along, uncaring except for her innate contempt for mean laziness.

Going into the bakery by the front door, she saw the counter was nearly empty of the day's bread, and Ma Eriksen was wrapping up the last of the cinnamon buns in a sheet of old newspaper for the banker's wife.

"Good afternoon, Mrs. Coldstone," Ruth said. "Isn't it a lovely day?"

Mrs. Coldstone turned to stare at Ruth, then silently laid out a silver dime for the buns, nodded to Mrs. Eriksen, and waddled out the door, her head held unnaturally high.

"My goodness." Ruth laughed. "I must have forgot to wash my ears."

"All those ladies so upsy-yupsy, dey ban in all day whisperin' and rollin' der eyes like dey never had so much fun, talkin' about you," Mrs. Eriksen said in her strong Norwegian brogue. "You got to be careful off dem type a people."

"Because I finally threw that no good bum out the front door?" Ruth broke out into laughter. "I just wish I'da done it two months ago."

"Ya sure, but dem women, dey can cut you into little crumbs, even if dey full of *hestalörte.*"

"What's that *hestalörte?*"

Silver-haired Mrs. Eriksen looked over her shoulder and leaned over to whisper in Ruth's ear. "Horseshit."

"Oh, lady!" Ruth laughed. "Everything's going to be fine from now on!"

Riding as hard as they were, still Sam Paterson had time to think of the future. Once he'd put down Bobby's killer, he'd ride on north, taking Thomas along if that's what he wanted.

Then he'd break the bad news as best he could, and then he'd have to leave. Even if the old man held no bitterness toward him, he couldn't help feeling that he'd let down the one man he respected, even idolized, for he was much like the father he'd lost.

He couldn't stay there. He'd shrivel up and turn sour enough to pucker a hog's ass. Everytime he looked at the old man he'd feel like his saddle was slippin'.

—Just tell him slow, but tell him straight. Tell him you took care of the matter as best you could, then tell him good-bye, then hunt down Cookie and tell him if he ever sulled on the old man, you'll come back and cut him from crotch to brisket and let the gurgle out of him. Then pack your war bag and ride on west.

It was a bleak prospect. He had maybe a couple hundred dollars saved up, because there was always some stove-up broke-down cowhand along the way needing a hand, and he didn't ever count money as something worth saving.

The steel-dust was his one and only possession. Yet he was young enough and strong enough to get along without worrying about his old age. Old age would come along no matter what.

"Change horses," he called to the gangly Englishman bouncing along painfully in the hard leather saddle.

The horses were tired, but there was still an hour of daylight and Sam didn't want to waste it. They would eat in the night and rest. The horses wouldn't be as strong, but they'd make it through another day.

Once they reached Abilene, he'd buy 'em each a bushel of oats and a lollipop.

"Let's shorten your stirrups a notch," Sam said, seeing the wet stain on the seat of Thomas Lamb's overalls. "You can ease those sores some by putting your weight more on your legs."

"I dare say I'll survive. We British always carry on with a stiff upper lip and all that," Thomas Lamb said wryly. "All the same, I thank you."

Sam pulled a faded blue cotton shirt from his saddle back and handed it to Thomas. "Make a pad and slip it down inside your pants. Maybe save a little hide."

"I'll buy you a new one in Abilene, Sam," Thomas said, awed by the tenderness of the big cowboy.

"No matter. Let's ride."

The trail turned northeast, and at times, when Sam saw a herd ahead of them moving along as fast as the slowest steer, he aimed farther east and passed without being seen. He wanted no interruptions, no windy explanations, no nothing. He just wanted to go like a bat out of hell kicking rabbits out of the way.

They reached the banks of the Arkansas River toward dusk, bone tired, but Sam insisted on crossing.

"It's better campin' on the other side," he said. "All the drovers like to take their herds over in the mornings, so they always camp the night on this side."

"It seems a bit dark to swim a river where you can't see the other bank. And like most of my countrymen, I've not learned to swim."

"Just stay upstream of me, I'll have the rope to the other horses, and we'll get our butts cooled off some."

"I'd like that," Thomas Lamb said. "Let's go for a dip."

With that, they rode into the river side by side, splashing along strongly until the horses lost footing and were forced to swim.

In the darkness, Sam saw the sorrel moving down against him and he said, "Easy now, just hold his head up, he'll do the rest."

His calming, unhurried voice gave Thomas his confidence back, and he lifted the reins.

"Now, Thomas," Sam murmured, "just get off and hang on to the saddle horn like this." Sam lifted his boots from the stirrups and with one hand locked to the saddle horn and the other locked to the other horses' lead rope, he let the steel-dust make his own way. Thomas followed suit, and felt the sorrel rise and gain buoyancy.

"What a lark." Thomas laughed. "It's rather like a sleigh ride, is it not?"

"Whatever," Sam said. "It sure feels good to get a free wash."

In a few minutes they found an out-of-the-way camping place and Sam opened the watertight canister of Lucifers to start the fire.

Later on, after a dinner of fried meat and yesterday's cold corn dodgers, they stripped off their wet clothing and crawled into their blankets.

"We must've made a hundred miles today, maybe more," Sam murmured. "We ought to be in Abilene tomorrow late."

"Oh, if John Ruskin and William Morris could see me now." Thomas Lamb giggled a little hysterically.

"Never heard of them."

"They're the leaders of a group who think we all ought to get back to the earth and live by the basic truths of nature." Thomas Lamb's voice trailed off as he drifted into a deep and wholly natural sleep, drugged only by fatigue.

A hundred miles northeast across the great pasture, Abilene was girding up for the night. The streets were filled with drovers from the cow camps preparing to deliver their beef or having already delivered it and been paid off. The punchers were already on their own, ready to squander their year's wages on a few nights of glorious pleasure before returning to Texas and the ass end of a cow.

The high boardwalks were crowded with punchers moving from one saloon to another, looking for the loudest place with the prettiest sporting girls and the hell with everything else.

An occasional six-gun went off as some puncher tried to bring down the moon, and as the night went on, the cowboys took to crying out their brags, something they would never think of doing on the trail where any untoward sound might start the wild longhorns to running.

"Look out! I'm a hoss ne'er was rode!"

"I can walk like an ox, run like a fox, swim like an eel, and make love like a mad bull!"

"Bucker, fighter, wild-horse rider!"

"Give me a bucket of bull blood, give me the prairie grass!"

"I'm from Coleman County, Texas, where the screech owls roost with the chickens!"

"Look out, when I lay aholt, I'm a turtle that don't let loose till it thunders, by God!"

A sheriff and deputy moved through the crowd, reminding folks to conduct themselves at least halfway civilized, that is, don't throw up on the floor and don't piss in the street.

Whenever these rules were broken the cowboy went to jail, and by midnight the jail was full.

In the Blue Elephant Saloon, which boasted the longest bar in Kansas, Elam Stark nosed along through the noisy punchers like a blind dog in a meathouse, picking up a coin here and there or snaffling them off the bar, cadging drinks, and mentioning the charms and desires of his sporting girl, Dolly, who when not otherwise occupied sat at a table near the bar, wearing white feathers and sparkling bangles over her red satin dress cut low to reveal breasts the size of watermelons.

As she sat cradling a glass of nonalcoholic liquor, a very drunken cowpuncher staggered by, gaining two steps and losing one as he tried to reach the bar for a drink he imagined he needed. Doing his back-and-forth shuffle before the seated Dolly, he peered down into her magnificent décolletage and shifted his quid, thinking that this must be the spittoon civilized folks were supposed to use.

On that account, with solemn decorum, he spat a great stream of amber into Dolly's cleavage, and that was the end of his night, because a very rough man with a flattened nose had him by the collar and careened him out the front door, where he hit his head on the hitch rail and stayed out of trouble for the rest of the night.

Dolly, cursing like a river rat, stormed up to her cubicle, washed off the tobacco juice, and changed her dress to one in which she'd embroidered the brands of every cowboy who'd given her a tip extra. Then, with a few dashes of musky perfume, she came down the stairway to the cheers of every cowhand who recognized the brand of his outfit.

That dress was a winner.

A wild-eyed puncher met her at the last step and checked her dress for his brand. "No, we ain't there, Dolly!"

"Buy me a drink, cowboy?"

"Hell, yes, beggin' your pardon for cussin', ma'am."

Sitting down alongside her at the table, the wild-eyed cowboy threw out a twenty-dollar gold piece to pay for the drinks and said, laughing, "We're goin' upstairs, and I'm goin' to put my brand on you."

There was something extra crazy in his crazy eyes, even to Dolly's weak vision, and she asked, "What is that brand that I never heard of, cowboy?"

Dipping his finger into his whiskey he wrote on the table top:

$$2 \, N \, P$$

"You got me cowboy, I never seen that brand yet and if you don't mind my braggin', I seen a helluva lot of brands over a period of time."

He threw his head back and hooted. "Come on upstairs, I'll explain it."

Calculating, she decided she could handle even him, and went up the stairs again.

Inside her cubicle she slipped off the dress and her shift and beauty accessories, while the crazy-eyed cowboy gulped and stared at the full-blooming figure emerging.

"Now, cowboy," Dolly said coming to the bed where the puncher sat dumbfounded. Unbuttoning his new striped shirt, she said, "Tell me about your brand."

"Oh, gosh, Dolly," he said, blushing, "I can't. It ain't proper."

"Whisper it in my ear," she said, tossing his shirt in the corner and attacking his belt.

He leaned forward, closed his eyes, put his lips to her ear, and whispered, "Too lazy to pee."

"Hoooie!" She guffawed. "Head 'em up and move 'em out!"

Downstairs, Elam Stark noted Dolly's activities and mentally kept track of the money he'd expect at the end of the night. If it wasn't for that brand-embroidered dress, she'd have had a nothing of a night. She was just too damned fat. Even the most blind drunk of cowboys would pick a slimmer girl than her if there was one available, and there were about thirty in town that would outclass Dolly.

Might as well admit it and put her to scrubbin' floors in rich folks' houses.

He picked up another free drink some cowboy had gone off and forgotten and downed it so fast it wasn't noticed except by the bartender.

"Get yourself killed that way some night," the bartender muttered, taking the empty glass and mopping the bar.

"I ain't bought a drink in some years." Elam grinned although he felt insulted. "And I'm still here doing the same old thing."

"Fine by me." The bartender shrugged his shoulders and slyly poured a drink for himself under the bar without changing expression.

Got to get a new girl, Elam thought, his foggy mind coming to rest on his favorite fantasy. Get a new one, a real sweetheart, and take the stage to San Francisco. Pick up a few double eagles along the way. Maybe in San Francisco, he could run his badger game. That had worked well in Boston. Couldn't work it here. Only the banker and the preacher cared about their reputations, and neither one of them would get caught in the badger game.

That goddamned kid! That sonofabitch of a bitch of a Ruth! She was the one to work the badger. She could coo to some older banker in San Francisco, get his clothes off, and in comes the good old private detective, Elam Stark, notepad in hand.

Make him pay forever, first of the month on the dot, one hundred dollars. You get ten of them payin', you're knocking down a thousand a month. That bitch could line up a hundred of those swells if she'd only work.

Her problem is she's never been gored.

What she needs is to ride a picket, make her bleed.

What she needs is the butt end of a bullwhip right up the old T slot.

Break her. Break her good. Break her to please a man.

Setting his derby at a jaunty angle, he stroked his pencil-thin mustache and wondered where he could steal a blacksnake whip.

Just down the street at the bakery, the two women worked in the back room with the front door locked. The dough for tomorrow's bread had been kneaded, had risen, been punched down, and was rising one more time before the pans would go into the big iron ovens.

Both wore full aprons, and their perspiring faces were dusted with flour. With both doors closed, they could hardly hear the hoo-raw outside while they worked the dough with care and concentration.

Mrs. Eriksen had made a sorghum roll with syrup and sweet spices, then cut off inch-wide pieces and laid them in a flat pan. They would use up the last of the oven's heat after the bread was done.

"Sometime, I want to bake nothing but cakes." Mrs. Eriksen chuckled. "I'd use a dozen eggs in each one, and a pound of sugar besides. Wouldn't that be something!" She smacked her lips joyfully.

"I was thinking we could bake cookies, a whole bunch of them, and sell them by the dozen to the drovers and sort of remind them of home."

"Ya, dat's a good idea," Mrs. Eriksen said, "but where do we find time? Dat's da problem. I'm tired after the bread."

"But I haven't anything else to do. Why don't I stay an extra hour or two and make some gingersnaps?"

"Wal, we got da ginger and I got a heckuva recipe, but if you work extra, you got to be paid extra, too."

"Whatever you say." Ruth smiled.

"You better ban be thinking of taking over," Ma Eriksen said seriously. "My ankles is givin' out. Dey swell up like popovers every morning, ya."

"Let's find you a chair. Or a stool would be better so you can sit while you're working."

"It's an idea, Ruthie." Ma Eriksen wiped her forehead tiredly. "Don't think I don't appreciate what you're doing."

"If you want to go home to bed I can finish up," Ruthie said, concerned that Ma Eriksen was driving herself too hard.

"Ya. Maybe you got somethin' der alright." Ma

Eriksen blinked her eyes and took off her apron. "Ain't nothin' left except take out the bread when is done. If you want to make the cookies while you waitin', go ahead, and they ban be yours to eat or sell or give away."

"Thank you, Mrs. Eriksen."

"You know," Ma Eriksen said somberly, "I was baker for the king and queen of Norway, and I could make a cake as high as I could reach, with flags and lettering and everything on it, but then I met Bernard. Ach, quit the job, go to the new country on a dirty boat. Ride a train to nowhere full of crazy cowboys and Indians . . . oofda . . ."

"Why?" Ruth asked the old lady.

"Why, ach, why?" Mrs. Eriksen rolled her eyes and chuckled. "Because, Ruthie, I love dat Bernie."

A tall, heavily built man carrying a cane with an ivory handle limped off the train. Clean shaven, he wore a rich beaver hat low over his eyes. Except for the limp, he walked with an imperious air, as if he'd just finished building a canal and was ready to start a railroad.

He inquired of the drayman which was the best hotel in town, and when advised that the Abilene Ritz was brand-new, he asked to be taken there with his baggage.

The tip was small.

"Please give me your best suite," the big man told the wide-awake clerk.

"Number ten is four dollars . . ."

"I'll take it," the stranger said, hanging his cane over his left wrist.

In a few minutes, Raven Dermott was settled in a large room that was somewhat crowded with heavy, ornately carved black walnut furniture not really necessary to his life, but which made him feel as if he possessed everything in sight.

He was tired from the trip and preferred to be fresh and sharp-witted when he went out to find his prey. There was no hurry. If she were here, he would find her easily enough. If she'd moved on, he'd still find her.

Uncorking a bottle of Spanish brandy, he drank directly from the bottle, then held it to the light. The finest for the finest, he smiled, pleased that he'd eluded any pursuers and could start afresh once again. This time, he promised himself, he wouldn't gamble, he would simply take whatever he turned up.

The first thing he would take would be Ruth Campbell.

Undoubtedly, there were no flowers in town to make a bouquet, and whatever sweets would be old and stale. What possible gift could he give her as a token of things to come?

In his bag he carried five yards of Irish lace, as well as various spools of colored satin ribbon, always a favorite with the ladies.

Then he had a few breast pins, finger rings, and a very fine Spanish shawl. After that, he would give himself.

Start with a yard of lace. Ocher or white? White, of course, for purity.

Undressed, he lay in bed by lamplight, smoking a long cheroot. He felt tempted to ask the clerk for a young sporter, but he fell asleep while he was thinking about it.

Elam passed through the livery stable quietly, if a little unsteadily. What sound he made was muffled by the stamping of horses in their stalls. He found the bullwhip with the two-handed hickory stock covered by braided buckskin as he'd remembered, even with the little tassel on the end.

That'll be nice, he thought happily, slipping the coiled whip under his coat and passing on into the alley.

Patting his derby, he veered his way down the alley, thinking, by God, it's time to show her what loyalty means. Shouldn't have been so easy on her. That's your trouble, Elam, you're too kind and gentle. You let them good nauches take an inch, they'll steal a mile. Put your foot down this time. Give her a taste of her own medicine, he thought happily, uncoiling the whip and using both hands, practicing the long layout on a trash barrel.

Pretty good, Elam. Pretty damned good. You'd make a mule skinner blush, by God, and you'll scrape that woman so bad her ma wouldn't know her from a fresh beef hide.

She'd be just leaving the bakery about now. Take her there? Or wait till she's down at the house getting ready for bed? House better. Don't have to drag her. Take her clothes off. Pop her with the whip. Bring her to her knees. By God, Elam, why didn't you think this up a long time ago? I'm goin' to just lay there with her after I knock her on the head, just goin' to lay there with her, with the lamp down low, and then I'm goin' to spit on the butt stock of this here whip and see how much she can take.

Oh, goodness me, we goin' change things for the better. We goin' to San Francisco. We goin' to get the old badger to payin' our way to a mansion on Nob Hill.

8

A thin wafer of lavender dawn lay over the low river valley as Ruth made her way home. She felt tired, but she also felt the pleasure of having given full measure to her work, and she expected to be paid accordingly.

As badly as she'd botched her life so far, she thought there was still a sliver of hope if she gave it her best shot. Even in her wildest dreams as a child, she had never thought she'd become a professional baker, but here she was, on her way.

She found her key to the front door and turned the lock. As she opened the door, Elam Stark, waiting inside in the darkness, struck with the heavy butt of the whip, the blow catching her on the side of her face, knocking her to her knees.

"Now, woman, you're goin' to learn respect for your husband," he growled.

"You're not my husband," she gasped, "and I'll never respect you."

Using the stock of the whip as a club, he hit her

again, and as she tried to scream for help, he swung a third time and dealt her such a blow to the side of her head she collapsed to the floor unconscious.

"Now, my dear bride," Elam Stark said softly, "if you don't know respect, I guess you're not too old to learn."

Putting the bullwhip aside, he lifted her by the shoulders, dragged her into the tiny bedroom, and flopped her on the iron bedstead.

As he stopped to get his breath, Ruth's mind started to clear, but she didn't open her eyes or make any movement. She was confident that in an even fight, she could win, but he'd been clever enough to use the club and take her by surprise.

Now she must use whatever wits she had left in order to get away from him.

If she only had a gun!

But there was nothing like a weapon in the bedroom. The butcher knife was off in the kitchen.

"Now, little wifey, I'm goin' to get my partner Mr. Bullwhip, and we're goin' to consummate this here marriage."

Turning, he shambled into the front room and retrieved the whip.

She tried to rise, but dizziness overwhelmed her and she fell back to the blankets.

"I just don't think you're goin' to make fun of Elam Stark again," he muttered, slipping his suspenders down to hang over his fat hams and unbuttoning his shirt.

After removing the shirt and tossing it in the corner, he went ahead and unbuttoned the top half of his greasy long johns and pulled his arms out of the sleeves, letting the garment droop down from his waistband. His upper body was pale and flaccid, his fat hairless breasts drooping as if he were neither male nor female, but a neutered stag.

It was this feminine quality, which she'd misread as tenderness, that had turned her head, and although she hadn't been aware of it, it was this feminine quality of tenderness and gentility that she'd lost when her mother died and for which she sought without knowing even what it was she needed.

Stark's pink chubby cheeks shone with a film of sweat as he lay on the bed next to her and ripped the frock from bodice to hem, revealing only a heavy muslin petticoat.

"You bitch," he said, looking at her dark hawklike features, already swelling from the clubbing. "I'm goin to give you about a foot and half of prod, and I'm going to watch you enjoy it, too."

With that, he attempted to pull the shift up over her hips, but just as it seemed he'd worked it free of her weight and was bringing it up over her waist, she sprang sidewise and jabbed the first two fingers of her right hand into his eyes as hard as she could. As he screamed in pain, she eluded his groping hands and ran for the door.

She paused to think a moment. She wanted to run the two blocks to Mrs. Eriksen's house, but her dress was ripped so badly she'd create an instant scandal. The women would run her out of town for disturbing their peace, and she'd lose what precious little opportunity she had in the bakery.

Elam Stark staggered from the bedroom, squinting through his left eye but holding the bullwhip at the ready.

"Bitch!" he roared, and popped the whip across her stomach. She started for the kitchen, hoping to get the butcher knife, but he barred the way, and with a grin backed to the counter and grabbed the knife in his left hand, then advanced on her.

"You get in that bed," he yelled, his voice going high.

"I'm through with you," she came back strongly. "Leave me alone!"

As he came at her, she had no place to go except out the front door. Scandal or no scandal, she wasn't going to wait for him to beat her to death.

She backed to the edge of the front porch, facing Elam Stark, who was breathing hard again from the slight exertion.

"I'm going for the sheriff," she said.

"He'll just tell you to get married and save your reputation."

She backed down the steps, ready to run like a deer if he made a move at her, and slowly backed toward the front gate.

"Listen," she said, "put down that knife and the whip, and let me get dressed. Then we can talk."

"Come inside," Elam Stark grinned, "you'll catch cold out here with hardly anything on."

"I'm not coming near you until you put away the knife and whip."

"Yes, you are, my dear. You're goin' to do exactly what Elam Stark tells you to do."

The sun was well on the rise by now, and the townspeople were on the move from their homes to their businesses, but none happened to come up her street.

Just one good man, she prayed.

And as Elam Stark took another step forward, curling the whip popper around her bare feet, the man strolled around the corner, limping slightly and using an ivory-handled cane.

There he was, a gentleman in a frock coat and beaver hat out for his constitutional, suddenly caught in the middle of a family dispute.

It was a grim sight, what with the half-naked Elam Stark looking like a fat pickled corpse and the dark-haired girl in dishabille, her face swollen, the bruises turning purple.

What else could a gentleman do?

"I beg your pardon. May I be of assistance?" he asked Ruth, ignoring the corpulent Elam Stark.

"I just don't know how," she said, drawing her torn bodice together. "My clothes are in the house."

"Sir," the gentleman said, "put aside your weapon and permit this lady to dress."

"Get the hell out of here. This is my house, and she's mine."

Raven Dermott's mind was running at top speed. He hadn't expected to be anywhere near so lucky. He'd just come walking this way after asking the hotel clerk directions to Ruth's home.

And this was the house. The girl had to be Ruth. Except for the dark complexion, she even resembled her brother. On top of it all, there stood Elam Stark, who was the only obstacle to his plan.

He would have much rather waited and played it out over a period of days, but the opportunity was too good to resist.

After hesitating a few seconds, double-checking the pieces in his game, he opened the gate and said to Ruth, "Would you permit me to escort you to the front door?"

"He's dangerous. That knife is no toy," she warned.

"Just say yes," he smiled.

"Yes, sure. If you think you can handle that damned tub of guts."

"Rotten nauch!"

Elam Stark roared and took another step forward, menacing her with the knife.

Raven Dermott casually reached inside his frock coat, brought out a single-shot .45 caliber derringer, and shot Elam Stark between the eyes at such short range the flesh was burned black around the wound.

Elam Stark collapsed like a stuck hog, his eyes rolled upward.

"Now then, go inside and get dressed," Raven Dermott said calmly, admiring the precision of his shot. "Don't touch anything, I'll go for the sheriff."

It had all happened so smoothly and quickly, she could hardly believe it. It seemed like a bad dream from which she'd awaken at any moment, but he touched her shoulder to break the spell, and she moved around the body and went inside the house like a sleepwalker while Raven walked up the street to find the sheriff standing on the boardwalk in front of his office.

"Good morning, Sheriff, I'm sorry to disturb you, but I just shot a man, and I think you'll probably want to investigate it."

"Shot a man? Who?" The sheriff asked indignantly.

"I don't know his name. He's rather fat and lives in a white house two blocks over with a picket fence around it. The lady there is dark-complected, and her face is badly bruised."

"That'd be Elam Stark, the fool. Let's go."

The sheriff mounted his horse, while Raven Dermott strode along, favoring his left leg but holding his head high as if enjoying the fresh air.

The scene was exactly as it had been, except that Ruth stood on the front porch wearing a different calico frock.

The sheriff nudged the body with the toe of his boot. "Close range."

"Yes, he came at me with the knife. I told him to stop, and when I could wait no longer, I fired."

It wasn't as simple as that, Ruth thought, but the man is making it that way so the sheriff won't have any call to arrest him and go to a lot of bother for nothing.

"No question he had the knife and the bullwhip. No question he was short a little furniture in the upstairs parlor, and you sure had no call to shoot a perfect stranger except in self-defense."

"I felt, too, that I was defending the lady. After all, she'd obviously suffered a terrible beating."

"But that's none of your business."

"I suppose that's correct out here in the wild West, but in the East women are not clubbed or stabbed by brutes!"

"This ain't the East, remember that, mister," the sheriff said, sizing up the bulky, well-dressed gentleman. "What might be your business here?"

"I came in on the train yesterday; I'm in the land development business, representing a group of investors in Philadelphia."

"All right," the sheriff said, duly impressed. "I reckon you can go on about your business. I'll send the meat wagon down for the body."

"Thank you, Sheriff. It's been a pleasure seeing you handle the problem so quickly and fairly."

"I'm just doin' my job." The sheriff stood a little straighter, acknowledging the praise.

As the sheriff left, Raven Dermott went up on the porch and gently took Ruth's hand.

"I'd be proud to be of service to you, madam."

"I'm some mixed up just now," Ruth stammered. "I don't know what I'm doing or where I'm going."

"I understand. Yesterday you were a housewife, today you're a widow. May I ask if you have funds enough to tide you over this sad business?"

"I never married him or nothing," Ruth said. "I've got a job at the bakery, or I did."

"Did?"

"I can't work there anymore. Mrs. Eriksen would go broke. The ladies in this town are . . ."

"Intolerant." Raven smiled knowingly. "Never mind, my dear, I'm sure you can weather the storm."

"I don't know. Last night I thought I had it figured out, then he come at me with the butt of the whip, and everything just went to hell in a handbasket all over again."

"It happens, madam, I'm buying a buggy and team to carry me west so I can investigate investment opportunities in land. If you'd care to travel with me, I'd be deeply honored."

She looked into his face and saw nothing amiss. True, there were downside grooves beside his mouth that belied the hearty smile on his face, and it was hard to see into his eyes the way her dad had told her to do, but compared to Elam Stark, he was a fine man of heroic proportions.

"I'm sorry," she said, "but it wouldn't be proper."

"I know what you mean, but believe me, I would not invade your privacy in any way, and I would appreciate someone to talk to."

She knew she was finished in Abilene. Now she was not only ostracized by the "better element" in town, she was also fair game for any man with a bag of tricks.

They would lie, they would cheat, they would pretend, they would offer marriage, a fortune, but if she were stupid enough to yield to any of them, they would consign her to the life of a whore.

She'd learned that much from her time in Abilene. No longer was she a starry-eyed kid wanting to see the Elephant.

"Let me think on it some," she said. "I'm tired and mixed up just now."

"Very well, I only want to help," Raven said. "I'm leaving for Colorado in about four hours. If you should change your mind, I'll be at the Hotel Ritz."

"Colorado?" she asked, surprised. She'd thought he was talking about western Kansas or eastern Nebraska.

"Yes, ma'am. It's a long journey. And as I said, you would have complete privacy in every way."

"You mean like two hotel rooms? Is that what you're saying?"

"That is exactly what I'm saying." He smiled and patted her shoulder paternally. "Perhaps you know the area and can be of some service."

"I know it. I rode it. I was born up there," she said.

"Say no more, please. I'll understand if you don't care to go, but believe me, you're most welcome."

With that, he touched the brim of his beaver hat and left her to plan a new life.

She stayed inside when the makeshift hearse came and the mortician and his helper loaded up the body and quietly departed.

She looked in the mirror and saw the lumpy bruises on her face, and she knew she could no longer stay in Abilene.

She looked in her purse and found a dime and a nickel. So she had only what Mrs. Eriksen owed her, which wasn't enough to carry her from nowhere to nothin'.

The house rent would come due next week.

There was nothing to keep her here in Abilene.

Mrs. Eriksen would lose her business if she tried to

buck the pecking order. Nowhere, no nothing, that's Ruth Campbell.

Her haunted eyes looked back at her in the mirror, and suddenly they flooded with unbidden tears.

Damn it, why did I have to be such a cocky smart aleck?

Why didn't I just listen to Pa and Sam and Bobby?

While she pondered her future, the bulky stranger was at the livery barn inspecting horses. No longer the dapper city gentleman, he'd taken off his coat and was running his hands over the neck of a black Morgan, seeking out any hidden lumps. Then he forced open the horse's mouth and checked the teeth. The livery-man had said the gelding was six, but he was eight. No matter. Squatting beside the horse he ran his hands down both front legs to the hoof, looking for shin buck or ringbone, but so far he was sound.

Lifting the hoof backward between his legs, he checked for cracks and dug a dull knife into the frog, cleaning out the manure, then he bent close and smelled it for thrush. So far so good.

The liveryman realized he was up against an expert and was already discounting the price he'd first thought to ask.

"Fair old horse," Raven said, going to the matched mate. They were so closely matched in size and conformation they might have been twins and probably were full brothers.

Weren't twins, because this one was seven years old, but he checked out well except for a scar across his pastern, probably caused by clipping a rock or almost anything.

It seemed to be well healed.

"That leg looks bad," Raven said, beginning the dealing.

They leaned on the fence rail and discussed this and that aspect of horses in general and these two in particular until the money started to become close to final.

"I wouldn't take a cent less than four hundred for the pair, mister," the liveryman said tightly, already feeling he'd been slickered.

"Sweeten the deal with a set of harness, and you've made a sale."

"No, sir. Can't do that. Here's the way it lays out. The team is four hundred. The harness is a hundred fifty. The buggy is two hundred and away you go."

"You've got to do better'n that. Cash money's tight nowadays."

"Seven hundred," the liveryman said, starting to walk away.

"Done," Raven Dermott said, smiling to himself.

Paying over the money and taking the bill of sale, he drove the harnessed team over to the hotel and tied them to the hitch rail.

"I'll be checking out at twelve sharp," he said to the clerk, and went to his room to pack his bag.

She'll come, he thought, she has to. Offer her all the slack she wants, sing her a love song, give her a yard of Irish lace, and then pick the plum right off the tree.

He asked the clerk to stow his bag in the trap of the buggy and sat on a horsehide sofa in the lobby cleaning his fingernails.

He hardly recognized her when she came in the door carrying a pair of buckskin saddlebags over her shoulder.

On her feet were scuffed bulldogger boots especially made for her small feet, blue jeans rolled up, a checkered flannel shirt, a red-and-white-splotched cowhide vest with the hair on and silver conchas for buttons, and sitting firmly on her long black hair was a flat-topped wide-brimmed Stetson that had carried a lot of water and fanned a lot of fires.

It was the same outfit she'd worn the day she'd run off from Paradise Valley.

Her hair was loose so that most of her bruises were shaded, and she walked with a newfound confidence, perhaps a result, he noted, of the sheathed bowie knife hanging from her broad belt.

"My goodness, my dear," he said, rising and touching his hat, "what a transformation."

"I'm ready," she said.

"Then let us depart. I have a lot of ground to cover in too short a time."

"Good-bye, Abilene," she said, stepping up into the buggy.

"And no hard feelings," he added with a smile.

From now on, she was his, and Paradise Valley was his. She just didn't know it yet.

Still far to the south, Sam Paterson and Thomas Lamb were beating across the prairie as fast as they could ride without killing their horses. Already they were down to half the speed of the day before and it didn't seem to matter much how often they changed their relay mounts. They were all tired.

Sam estimated they were no more than twenty miles outside of Abilene by the time the sun had full set and darkness rose out of the tall grass.

As much as he wanted to continue, he didn't dare push the horses any further. There could be a prairie-dog village hidden in the darkness just waiting to snap a good horse's leg, there could be a coulee or a cutbank that you couldn't see until it was too late.

They found a little seepage in a slough where

Thomas dug out a drinking hole for the horses, and after it had cleared, he filled their canteens.

With the tiniest of fires, they warmed the meat, chewed, swallowed, and fell onto their blankets like dead men.

In the morning, Sam discovered the old packhorse had gone lame, and he turned the animal loose. With rest, it might heal in a week. There was plenty of grass and water. Sooner or later he'd pick up with another cavvy.

He cinched down the pack saddle on one of the big brutes taken from the Liverpool boys and came back to the fire, where Thomas was frying sowbelly and corn dodgers.

"What time do we arrive?" Thomas asked.

"About noon, probably," Sam said. "I just wish we could have made it in yesterday."

After eating and making sure the packs were secure, they mounted and rode more slowly northeast.

There were Texas cattle herds about, but Sam avoided them. They were all going to the same place. Sam prayed they would beat Raven Dermott into town, not knowing that they were already a day late.

His Remington .44 was oiled and loaded, his Spencer carbine the same. Whatever happened was out of his hands, and worrying wouldn't change anything.

"What you aim to do in Abilene?" Sam asked the thin Englishman scrooching around, trying to find a soft place on the saddle.

"I thought I might look over the gardening prospects. The land looks quite bountiful."

"You'd sell your truck and greens to the folks in Abilene?"

"Who else?"

"That's it. There isn't anyone else, and I'd guess

most of the women have a poke patch in their backyards right now."

"That would be unfortunate."

"This is cattle country. Maybe best you changed over from truck to beef."

"I'd rather be in touch with the earth directly, not through feeding a cow," Thomas said straight-faced. "We have to return to the veritudes of nature, otherwise our whole world will collapse."

"I don't even know how big this pasture is, let alone the world." Sam grinned.

"It does make a serious man look a trifle silly," Thomas said wryly. "In England, one gets back to the land by renting a little garden space inside high stone walls, and then one goes to spading and raking."

"Then you set around a table half the night talking about thrips and sowbugs, I reckon," Sam said.

"No, we sit around discussing the future of our movement, how many believers have joined the brotherhood."

"Brotherhood?"

"Yes, the Pre-Raphaelite brotherhood. It's a group of thoughtful men, mostly artists, who live in Europe and want to get rid of all the frills and decorations for decorations' sake and return to the reality of our planet."

"I'd go along with that. Like these women wearing ostrich feathers, now. What's the sense in that? They don't keep anybody warm, and all they do is get in the way. Better they stayed on the ostrich."

"Yes." Thomas laughed. "The poor naked ostrich is walking around with his nose dripping, freezing his behind, while these foolish women are tickling each other's noses with his feathers and sneezing."

"And I've seen men with a stiff collar so high, they had to mount a soapbox to spit," Sam said.

"That sounds like my older brother." Thomas laughed, and talking through his nose commenced mimicking his brother. "Hear hear, my fellow Lords, let us send the Irish to Australia and the wogs to Ireland, thereby solving the problem."

"Hear hear!" Sam chuckled. "Don't you ever want to go back?"

"Lord love a duck, no. Somewhere on this great continent is a life for me."

9

Riding into Abilene in the early afternoon, Sam and Thomas looked no more wild and trail-worn than most newcomers except those who conveniently alighted from the train with hardly more than a few cinders dusting their clothes.

True, Thomas was half standing in the stirrups, his butt skewed, testing for saddle sores with every little rise and fall of the saddle.

Unshaven, red-eyed, layered with various colors of caked dust, lean and ornery from the steady diet of a wolf, they resembled most other waddies arriving from the south.

Stepping down from their horses and tying the string to the hitch rail, the first thing Sam Paterson could think of doing was to remove his hat, whack a cloud of dust off it against his thigh, then plunge his head clear to his shoulders into the wooden trough full of cool, clear water.

Coming up for air, he smiled and said, "By God,

that felt so good, I'm going to have another one," and again ducked his head, and scrubbed his face as he did so.

Thomas was not long in following suit, and after they were refreshed, Sam said, "Now maybe we better twist the bull's tail."

Unobtrusively settling his Remington revolver on his hip and making sure it wasn't hard jammed into its holster, Sam looked up and down the street, saw the Abilene Ritz Hotel sign, and turned that way.

"A room with two bunks," Sam told the clerk, "and a couple tubs. Then maybe you can buy us a couple new rigs." Sam laid out an extra twenty-dollar gold piece.

"The tubs are down the hall at the back. You're early, you can have the room next to the bath," the clerk said, staring at Thomas's bib overalls.

"Much obliged," Sam said, and, carrying his war bag, walked down the hall, unlocked the door, and saw the two half beds and two ewers of water sitting in big china basins.

"First thing a bath, then some new clothes, and then start looking for Ruth, and we'll visit the barber and then we'll eat," Sam said, throwing his bag into the room and continuing on down the hall to the bathroom.

Hot water simmered in copper boilers on a wood stove, and the two copper tubs, which closely resembled high-sided coffins, stood on either side.

Dipping water from a boiler and pumping in enough cold to make it tepid, Sam crawled in the tub and let his body laze and soak for a few minutes, and Thomas, after gently peeling off his overalls and the soft spare shirt from his sitter, did likewise.

"I've got some bear grease that'll fix up your blisters

in a jiffy. Won't work if you're sweaty and dirty and riding hard, but you'll be ready as a hog butcher in frost time soon enough."

"I dare say I could stand a little relief." Thomas smiled as he soaked in the hot water and sudsed up a bar of cut yellow soap. "What are you going to tell Ruth?"

"Depends on how she is."

"You mean her health?"

"I don't rightly know. If she's right side up, I'll just tell her Bobby's gone. If she's lost her stirrups, maybe I won't."

"Lost her stirrups?"

"She went off with a skunk who was passing himself off as a government man from the East with a lot of extra irons in the fire. If she straightened him up, she's got my blessing, but if he's run her down, then I aim to play it some different."

"She means a lot to you, doesn't she, Sam," Thomas said quietly.

"I reckoned she was about the only hope I had for changing pastures. I'd have gone on to California after she flew off with that hombre, but her dad needed a little something more'n a hired hand about that time."

"I understand," Thomas said. "Perhaps she and that man will be ready to return to Paradise Valley and take over."

"I just doubt if Elam Stark could pour piss out of a boot if'n it was full and upside down," Sam said, and started scrubbing his long, hard-muscled body, putting an end to his unusual loquacity.

A knock at the door, and the clerk entered with a bundle of new clothes, which he arranged in two piles.

"If they don't fit, let me know," he said, and left them alone again.

"I'm about due for a new set of boots and a hat," Sam said, taking a coarse towel and drying off.

"I wonder that no one out West has yet thought of the pith helmet we use in India instead of the twenty-gallon Stetson."

"It won't wad up," Sam said.

"But it makes a perfect helmet when one falls off his horse."

"One don't fall off his horse out here. One might break a leg." Sam smiled.

Dressed, they looked like new men.

"That's some improvement," Sam said. "Now let's find that mule-headed woman."

" 'She was a phantom of delight, when first she gleamed upon my sight . . .' " Thomas quoted with a grin. "Whereaway, sir?"

"Find Stark. Start with the sheriff."

Stowing their old clothes in the room, the pair went out into First Street and located the jail and the sheriff's office.

Inside, resting easy in an oak swivel chair, they found Sheriff Cook nodding off after a hearty dinner of pork chops, mashed potatoes and gravy, coleslaw and dried-apple pie.

"Sorry to disturb your rest, Sheriff," Sam said.

"I thought I locked that door," the sheriff responded irritably.

"We just need a little information about a man name of Elam Stark," Sam said.

"Stark. That dumb bastard's planted on boot hill by now."

Sam sucked in his breath.

"When was that, Sheriff?" Sam asked carefully.

"Yesterday. Kilt in the morning, underground before sunset."

97

"Did he leave anyone behind to mourn?" Sam asked.

"I just doubt if she grieved much. She lit a shuck before we planted him."

"His wife, you mean?"

"What's all this about?" The sheriff became suspicious and got to his feet.

"Nothing, Sheriff. I'm an old friend of the family is all, and I was hoping to pay my condolences to his wife."

"What was her name?"

"Ruth Campbell before she changed it."

"That's her, but she never changed it. She took off with a high rollin' easterner about noon yesterday. Wasn't much else she could do. Wasn't proper company, you might say."

"How's that, Sheriff?"

"Livin' with that wet-legged moocher, she didn't have a chance, and with him dead, she had even less."

"I see." Sam nodded. "She say where they was headed?"

"Maybe. The Philadelphia lawyer outslickered Pete Wilson tradin' horses, took his best team and a buggy, and headed off for Denver. What's your interest in her besides friends?"

"I work for her pa. He's gettin' down and needs to see her while there's time." Sam lied badly. "He lost his son, and she's all he's got left."

"She showed some breeding. I'll say that for her." The sheriff nodded judiciously. "The fellow she went off with looked familiar in a way to me. I looked through my wanted posters but didn't find his picture."

"How'd he set up?"

"Big man, paunchin' up like a six-year bull, clean

shaved. Favored his left leg when he walked and carried a cane with an ivory handle. Dressed well, spent his money for his comforts. Know him?"

"No, reckon not. Thanks for your kindness," Sam said, and turned to leave, only to find two ranchmen coming in and barring his way. The older one carried a two-bore sawed-off goose gun and had it aimed at Sam's middle.

"Hold it," the older ranchman said.

"What is this, O'Brien?" The sheriff frowned.

"These rannies just rode in with Harry's horses."

"So that's it," the sheriff drawled, drawing his own six-gun covering Sam and Thomas.

"Wait," Thomas said. "I dare say I can explain."

"Remember we thought they was English, because they'd stopped at old lady Duncan's." O'Brien glared at Thomas.

"Rest her soul." The sheriff nodded.

"'Limeys,' she said, just before she went," the red-headed rancher said.

"There are quite a lot of British on the frontier, Sheriff," Thomas said. "And we've only just arrived."

"Riding Harry Halahan's horses. Hell, you can see the double H brand on 'em."

"We took them off three English hardcases," Sam said plainly.

"Where are they? Where's your bill of sale? I'm tellin' you, mister, you're goin' to answer for killin' the Halahans."

"I say, we've done nothing," Thomas protested. "What is this all about?"

"The Halahans was a young family trying to farm out east of town. Busted their butts out there, had good horses. When we found 'em, they'd been cut to pieces. Harry put up a fight, but took a big knife in the

99

back," the sheriff said. "Now just hand over your shootin irons, and back off down the hall to the cell. It's open."

"Sheriff, do you think we'd be crazy enough to sluice a whole family and come back with the evidence?" Sam asked.

"I'm going to check you out. If you're who you say, you're clear, but if you've got a blotted brand, I doubt we'd wait for a judge to come."

"Sheriff, I've got something better to do than wait for you to run through your fliers," Sam said quietly. "You can keep the horses for our bond. We'll be back within a week."

"Well, now I just don't know . . ." Sheriff Cook shook his head.

"I know!" The red-headed O'Brien growled, cocking both hammers on the two-bore. "Harry Halahan's wife was my daughter, and the kids were my grandchildren, and I'll blow you in two pieces, you try walking out of here, mister."

"That's it," Sheriff Cook said. "Now just don't make any sudden moves and you won't get hurt. Shuck that gun belt."

Sam, with a sinking feeling that he'd just lost his last hope, unbuckled his belt, let the holstered .44 drop to the floor, and walked down the hall with Thomas to the open cell door.

In a moment, the barred door clanged shut and the rancher said, "You better prove out, or you'll swing right soon."

"I say," Thomas said. "Don't you know that under common law a man is innocent until proven guilty?"

"Remember this, Englishman, I'd plug you both right now, if the sheriff would take a stroll somewhere."

"I hope I can return the favor, little man," Sam

Paterson said strongly. "Anybody as knot-headed as you ought to be cut and sent to Chicago."

"Big talk from a baby killer," the red-headed rancher blustered. "I'm goin' to delight in hearin' your neckbones pop."

"Look, three little ferrets had the horses. We only used them to come here," Thomas said. "They wanted to kill us as well."

"Not even a snake can lie better'n an Englishman," O'Brien snarled. "Saints preserve us."

"Look!" Thomas cried out. "Just because you're Irish and have a grievance against the English has nothing to do with the murder of your family. I promise you, that crime has been attended to by Sam."

"You killed three of the buggers?" the Irishman growled at Sam.

"They tried to ring us and I couldn't let 'em," Sam said.

"Where are the bodies?" the sheriff put in.

"About a hundred-twenty miles southwest of here if the buzzards have left anything."

"That's a hell of a fine yarn, but all we can see is the horses with a double H on their hips."

"I'd've brought their heads along had I expected this," Sam said. "Now you keep on callin' me a liar, I'm goin' to wool the lightnin' out of you and pound your iron head into the ground like a fence post."

"Bastard . . . you'll hang slow if I have anything to say about it," O'Brien retorted.

"O'Brien, I'm sorry about your troubles. It's no fun losin' your loved ones, especially if they ain't growed yet, but you are dead wrong and I'm goin' to sweat you for it," Sam said.

"Ah, you'll pay! You'll pay!"

"C'mon, Dad," the younger O'Brien said, "you're

just blowin' off steam, but you ain't turnin' any wheels."

"Listen, son, if I should be taken sudden, promise me these cutthroats will hang."

"I'll be there, Dad," the younger man said, glaring at Sam, "but it don't do any good just yammerin' back and forth."

"Sheriff," O'Brien said, "I'm holdin' you responsible."

"It's over, old man," Sam said gently. "I killed the runts after I give 'em warning. I wish I could've killed the men that made them that way, too. You ain't any different than them."

"You lie, bastard!" O'Brien stood back on his bootheels like a banty rooster and spoke in a deadly voice. "If you don't hang by tomorrow night, I'll be comin' in to do it myself."

"That's enough, O'Brien," the sheriff said, moving in between the old man and his prisoners. "Get on outside and cool off. These are my prisoners from now on."

Crossing the Kaw River at the confluence of the Solomon, the matched team brought the buggy smartly down the main street of Salina, which was occupied by sleeping dogs, stray chickens, and foraging pigeons. There was no proper Main Street, only a jumble of rickety buildings built without plan or direction.

On one of them was a crude sign: Rooms.

"I'm afraid we must accept what the country offers," Raven Dermott said, pulling up the team.

"A bed is all I need," Ruth said, hopping out of the buggy and securing the lead rope to the hitching post.

"Howdy there, folks," A heavyset lady with a bent back and bowed legs called, waddling out the front door. "What's your fancy?"

"Two rooms," Ruth said quickly.

"Two rooms is just exactly what I've got, not counting my lean-to out back," the old lady crowed. "Fifty cents a piece or seventy-five if I throw in your victuals."

"I don't suppose there's a restaurant in town?" Raven asked without hope.

"Right here. Grannie's Belly Packer. Goin' to put up the sign as soon as we can find some paint to do her."

"Sounds top chop to me." Ruth laughed. "I'm game."

"Then we'll stay," Raven said without enthusiasm.

"Don't worry about the horses. Grain and everything will be an extra fifty cents."

"For both?" Raven asked.

"Why, course not." The old lady laughed, revealing bare gums. "It's fifty cents for one. You want to have 'em both for fifty cents, we can divide the corn up between 'em."

"No, feed them both, we have a long way to go," Raven said tiredly, trying to be patient and bank his fire.

"Then light and set," the old lady crowed. "Tell me what's goin' on in the world. How's the price of beef?"

"I know nothing about the price of beef." Raven Dermott made a polite smile.

Inside, the house was divided into two rooms. One was the kitchen, with an iron cookstove and a plank table, the other barely held two beds divided by a blanket hanging from a pole rafter.

"You said two rooms." Raven pretended to object.

"I did," the old lady beamed. "Anybody trying to get through that army blanket in the middle of the night, I'll shoot to kill. Ain't that what you're payin' for?"

Ruth laughed at the old lady's humor and merry eyes while Raven tried not to sulk. He'd hoped to charm the girl over the slow passing miles so that she might be anxious to receive him, but it seemed every time he dropped his hand near her knee, she'd move aside, or a horse would fart, some damned thing.

And Ruth seemed to be such a part of the country in her riding outfit while everybody looked at him like he was a fresh-caught catfish ready to fry in his frock coat and stickpin.

Yet he dared not change his disguise. If they so much as guessed that he'd worked along the border, rustling cattle and horses, dealing cards, making his mark as an all-around deadly man, they'd connect up the rest of it, and he'd never see Paradise Valley.

Still, the passion was on him like a fire burning in his whole body. If he tried to put it out in his chest, it would move off to kindle heat on the skin, and if he tried there, it would erupt in his loins. It was like a six-horse team of wild horses stampeding.

He thought he knew his body's pleasure limits, and that he could maintain control, but there was a new power surging through his blood, poisoning his defenses, urging him to break out and take the girl as his own. After all, she'd been married, it wasn't that he was snatching a babe from the cradle. Even though she looked so innocent and childish, that worthless Elam Stark must have taught her every trick he'd learned along his devious way.

Maybe she was secretly suffering pangs of want for him, for the pleasure and fulfillment he could bring her, but she was too modest to be forward and give him the go-ahead.

After a supper of beans and fried pork, they went to their separate beds, but Raven couldn't sleep in the stuffy room.

God, she was right next to him, only the blanket in between. He thought he could hear her breathing heavily, and he felt his own body rise in answer. He thought he could smell her womanly fragrance, and he had to bite his knuckles to keep from whispering through the blanket. He thought he could feel her bed vibrate against his as she looked for a comfortable position for her young nude body.

He wasn't sure she slept in the nude, but it suited him to think so. It seemed like hours he waited until she was lulled into slumber, when he might lift the blanket and join into her dream without her realizing that she had her. Once the nail was driven, he would be too powerful to resist, and then she would give her all.

With these steaming thoughts cooking in his mind and raging through his loins, he waited until he could stand no more, then, carefully as a Boston burglar, he lifted the blanket, carefully, carefully. Not a sound, not a feather of disturbance.

Once he'd set the old wagon tongue in position, it would be a delirious ride. Once he touched her flank so that she would dream of a lover and parted her legs, he would lay it in.

His hand moved across the bed, seeking her fresh young hip, her lovely stomach, her, Christ almighty, her lovely nipples and melon breasts.

Ah, there she was. His fingers touched her skin as delicately as a safecracker's, and he smiled to himself. There was her bare hip, now to just stroke a little to bring her around and dream of the joy of life, to turn to him, and open wide for him, ah yes, it was such a mysterious magic in the darkness, as she responded to his caress, her breathing heavier.

In the passion of conquest he hardly touched her except to be sure she was positioned for his secret, almost furtive entrance, but once there, he drove the great old wagon tongue home with exuberance and authority, showing her once and for all who was boss. He felt her hands on his buttocks pulling him on, and he reacted like a mad bull, but still her hands gripped him tightly to her and he gave a great lunge that should have crushed her, saying "mine mine mine mine . . ." and she responded with the sweetest moaning a woman had ever given him.

Released, he lay like a coldcocked steer and drifted off to sleep, the conqueror, the master, the plunderer, and the new he-bear of Paradise Valley.

At dawn he awakened, feeling fine. She still lay quietly beside him, her breathing warm and sweet against his shoulder, and he wondered if he shouldn't give her another ramrod just to show her he could, but as he stroked her hair and touched her sweet haunch he felt something not quite right. The smooth peaches he'd expected were not so smooth.

He moved the hand ever so gently to her right breast, but it wasn't where it was supposed to be. Seeking, his hand found a hard, pug-nosed nipple hanging near her navel.

He opened his eyes then and in the dim light looked into Grannie's merry eyes.

"Good morning, love," she whispered, and bringing her right arm around his waist, pulled him close, puckered up her wrinkled lips, and said, "Care for another go, love?"

The breakfast of grits and sorghum was quiet, although Ruth tried to lighten the mood with sprightly small talk.

—Gosh, Grannie I slept like a log on a mountain. The lean-to was just like home.

—It's sure nice around here, I suppose it'll be a city of a thousand people if the railroad ever comes this far west.

—What a tasty breakfast, Grannie. You're a real magician. No wonder you have such a happy outlook on life.

"Ah yes, my dear," the old lady said, "the darkness in Kansas is a special kind."

"In what way, Grannie?" Ruth asked.

"It seems to bring out the best in men." Grannie smiled.

"We'd best be on our way," Raven Dermott muttered, having no appetite.

"Can't you stay a little longer?" Grannie asked, a ray of hope in her wrinkled smile.

"No, no. We're on our way to Colorado. That's a long way, you know," he stammered awkwardly.

Breathing a silent sigh of relief, Raven slapped the reins on the matched blacks and settled back in the overstuffed horsehide seat.

How much did she know? Had they cooked it up between them? Yet how? Damned women. How could they be so sneaky?

And did Ruth know all the story?

Did she know he'd pronged the old lady?

Or did the old lady just have her fun by herself?

Surely she wouldn't tell.

Thinking along these lines, Raven thought he might repair whatever damage was done by simple chitchat.

"I slept badly last night," he murmured, shaking his head as if trying to stay awake. "Even though you slept like a log."

"There wasn't a sound to disturb anyone. At least I heard nothing once I'd put my head down."

"Me too, for maybe an hour, and then I commenced having a nightmare."

"Too bad," she said sympathetically. "No wonder your eyes are so bloodshot and your face looks so tired."

"Yes, it was horrible," he said. "I dreamed a dragon had me in its embrace and it was breathing fire."

"Then what happened?"

"I don't know. I fought against it all night until I woke this morning in a cold sweat."

"Perhaps tonight you'll be more tired," Ruth said.

10

Pacing the floor of the cell, Sam banged his hands together in frustration.

He tried the bars again and they yielded no more than before. He looked up at the barred window in the wall above the bunks, but it was so small he couldn't squeeze through it even if it had no bars.

The rest was country-fired brick.

Scratched with a piece of white chalk rock on one wall was a souvenir from past times: JOE BAD, and underneath that written with a burned stick: THEY HUNG HIM, and underneath that in pencil: JOE BAD NO MO.

"Bit of a pickle," Thomas Lamb said, for want of anything else to relieve the tension.

"I'm sorry I dragged you into this," Sam said.

"I daresay it's my being English that's half the problem. O'Brien would rather hang an Englishman than beat his pig." Thomas made a smile.

"I'm more worried about that man Ruth's traveling with."

"Why?"

"It's too simple. Stranger comes to town, shoots her man, and off they go before he's even buried."

"It sounds as if she had few regrets."

"Maybe she's growin' up," Sam said, "but taking off with a stranger is about as smart as a flea with a big belly button."

"I suppose she needed help. Where could she ask?"

"I dunno. Maybe the preacher. He's supposed to be fair."

"But deep down, you know where the preacher is."

"I reckon most of 'em can't lick their upper lip unless the ladies vote on it."

"From what you've told me," Thomas said, trying to bolster Sam's spirits, "she can take care of herself pretty well."

"But she's still just a little girl," Sam protested.

"I don't think so. Little girls raised on a ranch must grow up rather quickly."

From the next block, they could hear the crowd in the Blue Elephant livening up. War whoops let loose by liquored-up punchers received an immediate response by others louder and more bloodcurdling.

A pebble sailed through the little window and rattled on the floor.

"What the . . . ?"

"Let me look," Thomas said, clambering up to the top bunk. From his full height he peered out the aperture.

"You there?" came a rasping voice.

"Yes, sir," Thomas said.

"Take this," the voice said, and Thomas hung his arm out the window only to feel a heavy revolver butt fitted into it.

"Why?"

"Your horses are in back," the voice rasped. "I'll try

110

to head those jaspers off, but I ain't so sure I can do it by myself."

Thomas heard the hoofbeats of a horse moving away swiftly.

"Who was it?" Sam asked, checking the loads in the Colt .45, making sure it wasn't some kind of a trap.

"I couldn't see him. He was standing on his saddle, I think. He said our horses were out back."

"It's somebody on our side at least," Sam said, slipping the long-barreled Colt in the back of his waistband.

Night was coming on, and the shadows in the street lengthened into darkness hardly illuminated by oil lamps in the saloons and store windows.

Inside the Blue Elephant, in the dim light, all the sporters looked like they were damsels with big wide eyes and lips like ripe cherries. Their costumes of feathers and satin with ruffles and glass beads made them appear to be enchantresses out of a fairy story.

The longest bar in the West was crowded with punchers bellying up, and in the center the red-headed banty rooster O'Brien stood on his toes and sang the spirited ballad "The Brave Donegal Boys":

> Oh the dogs in red,
> They shot the women down.
> Oh the dogs in red,
> They shot the children down,
> But the brave Donegal boys
> Rose like an emerald wave
> And sent the dogs in red
> Down to their boggy grave . . .
> Hurrah! *Erin go bragh!*

"And to think they'd follow us all the way to Kansas to slaughter the women and children!" he cried out.

"That's the way they are," O'Brien's son replied on cue.

"Does no one remember the Halahan family? Has their murder been forgotten and unavenged? Bartender, give us another round!"

"Sure, we remember," the son answered loudly.

"Does no one remember poor widow Duncan asettin' in her rockin' chair, and how they split her poor gray head just for a handful of silver?"

"Sure. She never hurt anybody."

"And the Halahans, the poor young couple finally finding freedom from the English tyrants only to see them coming with their sabers and iron bars. Give them credit, they went down fighting, but the wee babes, all the three of them, murdered in their beds, God rest their sweet souls."

"Who did it?" a puncher growled. "We don't allow things like that where I come from."

"The pair locked up in the jail did it. Can you believe the sheriff would've turned them loose hadn't I made such a fuss!"

O'Brien was becoming so involved in his drama that he commenced to make his story fit the way he felt no matter how far he strayed from the truth.

"There they were with the plunder, the horses, the silver, and blood on their hands! And that sheriff said he had to protect their rights!"

"What about the rights of the widow Duncan!"

"What about the rights of the Halahans!"

"What about simple plain ordinary American justice!"

"Hurrah! *Erin go bragh!*" O'Brien's son at the end of the bar roared.

"I tell you, those babes' blood cries out for justice!"

"Git 'em!"

112

"I've got the rope!" O'Brien yelled.

"Up the rope they go!"

"Necktie party! Bring the whiskey!"

Lost in fury, the mob of punchers, townsmen, and drummers poured out into the street.

Led by the cock sparrow O'Brien, who cradled his two-bore sawed-off goose gun in his left arm, and sided by his son, who wore his six-gun low, they advanced to the jail, where they encountered the old sheriff and a man wearing a strange badge on his vest.

"Hold it there, O'Brien," the sheriff yelled, raising up his old Dragoon, "you ain't taking my prisoners."

But the pressure of the mob was too much, and O'Brien was pushed up close to the sheriff.

"Give us the keys, Sheriff, and then you can take the night off," O'Brien commanded.

"I'm givin' you nothing, O'Brien, but I'm going to arrest you when your mob strays away and sobers up."

Inexorably the hooting and hollering lynch mob crowded forward.

"Stop it!" the man in the brown peaked hat yelled, drawing his six-shooter. "I'm a U.S. marshal, and I'll count three before I start shooting off the leaders."

Hardly had he spoken than young O'Brien blindsided him with the barrel of his Colt, dropping him like a rock down a well.

That was enough for Sheriff Cook.

"Don't hurt me, boys, I'm just trying to do my job," he whined.

"The keys!"

"On the nail behind the desk."

In went the elder O'Brien with his son coming close behind.

O'Brien took the key ring hanging on the wall and held it high. "Let's go, boys!"

Inside the cell, Thomas Lamb saw the choleric Irishman advancing and said, "Maybe you better start shooting, Sam."

"I thought you was against killing."

"That I am, especially when it comes to somebody killing me."

"We've got to get him close enough to get the keys," Sam said.

"You're always thinking ahead. Quite proper, Sam."

"Out you go, you murderin' scuts!" O'Brien yelled, holding the goose gun in his right hand now, aimed at Sam's head, the keys dangling in his left hand.

"Put the gun down, O'Brien, or I'll kill you!" Sam came back strongly.

"Oh, what brave talk from the murderer of babes! I might just blow your head off right now had I not promised the boys a party."

"I'm not playing party games, mister."

"Then you're mine, and the boys can have the Englishman." O'Brien grinned and slowly pressed the trigger.

"Down!" Sam snapped, and dropping to the floor, he pulled the .45 and shot upward into the pigeon breast of the red-eyed Irishman.

He grunted like a pig kicked in the butt, his fiery eyes bulging blankly. The goose gun rose and went off, sending its charge into the ceiling. O'Brien fell in a tormented heap.

"The keys!" Sam called to Thomas as he aimed the revolver at the younger O'Brien, who, instead of going to the aid of his father, was going for his gun.

Sam shot him in the chest, the heavy lead ball slamming him backward into the arms of the men behind.

Thomas had the bloody keys in his hand and

opened the iron barred door without coming into Sam's line of fire.

"Boys, you done made a big mistake, going against the law," Sam said levelly. "These two were wrong, mule-headed wrong about us, and now they're damned dead wrong. You all just back out of here and we'll join you in the Elephant for a drink in a minute."

The men in the hall spoke tersely to those behind them, and the mob moved like a wave, backward instead of forward.

In the street there was a scramble to get out of harm's way, which panicked those in front, as they felt deserted and betrayed.

"Hey, wait!"

"Where you goin?"

Suddenly, it wasn't a retreat, it was a rout, as even those in front had smelled the stench of fresh blood and knew they had no business being where they were. At any moment another bullet might come blasting out of that six-gun and the angel of death would sweep up another cowboy caught in his own loop.

They fell over themselves, scrambling to get out of the hall, and in a moment the way was clear except for the two bodies lying in a common puddle of blood already glazing over and turning black.

"Quick, friend," Sam said, grabbing from the wall his gun belt with its Remington .44 still loaded, then moving quietly to the back door.

"Here goes," he said, feeling like he was in a leaky boat ready to go over a waterfall.

Slowly opening the door, he looked out into the gloom and saw the steel-dust and the bay, fully rigged.

Still expecting a trick or an ambush, Sam sidled outside, keeping away from the light and watching for any movement.

There was nothing. The steel-dust stamped impatiently.

Sam swiftly mounted. In a second Thomas was beside him on the bay.

"We go slow," Sam whispered, holding up his hand, putting the steel-dust into an easy trot.

Staying in the alleys, they left the west side of town undetected as the mob slowly returned, a man at a time, slightly crestfallen or lying like jack mules that never stop braying.

They'd not expected the prisoners to buy a drink in the Blue Elephant, but it sounded like a good excuse to go on back there and let things settle down.

"Those damn O'Briens, always stirring up trouble."

"Finally paid for it."

"Gutshot the old pouter pigeon."

"Gave him a slimmin' lesson he won't forget."

"I popped a lot of caps, but them fellers had the devil's own luck."

"S'pose we ought to go after them?"

The group stared at the speaker silently until he turned away and said to the bartender, "I reckon I'll have another."

The sheriff had his hands full reviving the U.S. marshal without worrying about the two bodies lying in his hallway.

—Damned O'Briens, always carrying a chip on their shoulder. I told 'em, told 'em, and told 'em, but no, they got to show the world they're so tough. So tough they can take a ball in the belly and spit it back. Oh, yes, told 'em plenty times, don't mess in my business, you goin' to get hurt.

Frank Taylor, the marshal, groaned and felt the lump on his head, looked at his fingers for a sign of blood, and nodded.

"Hat broke the blow," the sheriff said, helping the marshal to his feet.

"I'll see that sonofabitch in a federal pen," the stocky marshal rasped.

"He's dead," the sheriff said. "His pa, too. Somehow the cowboy got a gun." The sheriff eyed the marshal's left holster, which was empty.

"If he hadn't had the gun, two innocent men would have been hanging, and the guilty ones would be back on their farms bustin' sod."

"I didn't say anything," the sheriff said. "I just live a day at a time and try to stay out of harm's way."

The marshal strode to the back door of the jail and looked out to see the horses gone.

"They made it," he said.

"You goin' after them? Want me to raise up a posse?"

"Better you clean up your mess and then play mumblety-peg with yourself," the marshal rasped, and strode out into the night.

"We never got to the barbershop," Sam said, scratching at the stubble on his jaw.

"I'm just thankful we're free," Thomas said.

"I reckon you're about as gritty as eggs rolled in sand. Good having you along," Sam said.

"British pluck!" Thomas Lamb laughed at himself as he noticed he was feeling overly proud. "All I did was fetch the key."

"You coulda dropped it." Sam smiled in the darkness and wondered if the sheriff was coming after them with a posse.

Didn't seem likely, the way the old man was washed out. Might have been a hell driver once, but he'd started worrying about his old age, and that had damped his powder. Better to just give your best run, and if you starve to death or freeze to death when you can't keep yourself no more, so much the better.

Don't give me too long a life, he asked the stars, just enough to keep me occupied and looking for more.

Salina was dark when they passed through. A couple of dogs ran out and challenged them, but they retreated once they'd said their piece.

"The prairie never stops," Thomas said, longing for a soft bed.

"We ought to come into Lincoln about dawn. We'll shake down there."

The trail west ran along the Kaw River, and an occasional small settlement would be situated along its banks in the places where the water could be directed into a mill wheel. Shady Bend, Tranquillity, Luther's Mill, none of which showed a light, being only lonely beginnings of dreams, and yet there was a sort of magic about the dark, solid buildings where people slept and made love and dreamed and died.

It worked both ways, Sam knew. The solitary family on the prairie could be exterminated by the dregs of humanity wandering loose, or a traveler could ask for a room for the night, and he would end up bashed in the head and et by the hogs with all his valuables hid under a rock in the hearth.

Such was the recent scandal of the Bender family down by Coffeyville, who had rented their spare room to eight different travelers before searchers found the remains of the bodies buried in the orchard. It was said that Kate Bender, who did the killing, was a believer in witchcraft. They all left before the law arrived and were never caught.

Travelers were both risky and at risk on the lawless frontier.

As they came up a low rise to a view of the Kaw

valley in the coolness of the dawn, they saw that Lincoln had its own Main Street planted to alfalfa and a few buildings on either side.

At the end of the street they found the Windsor Hotel, where Mrs. Lewis, an early riser, greeted them, and seeing the grim marks of exhaustion on their faces showed them to clean beds, where they shucked their boots and hats and fell asleep before they hit the blankets.

When they awakened a little before noon, they discovered that Mrs. Lewis had seen that their horses were fed and grained and that she'd held off cooking dinner until the men first ate their breakfast of grits, fried bacon and eggs with ponhaus and fried potatoes, and a piece of cream pie.

They were served by a little girl with golden curls named Pearl, and Sam felt a strange ache in his breast as the unbidden thought entered his mind suggesting it was time he started his own family before it was too late.

"Where's your pa, Pearl?" Sam asked.

"He left."

Just then Mrs. Lewis, a slender middle-aged lady, brought in a platter of cookies and shooed her daughter out of the room.

"If you want to know why Mr. Lewis left, I'll tell you."

"We don't mean to pry, ma'am," Sam said, blushing with embarrassment.

"Mr. Lewis left Lincoln because he said it was fourteen miles outside of the knowledge of God." She laughed. "And I'm so happy he's gone."

"To change the subject, ma'am, have you seen a heavyset easterner and a young lady about seventeen traveling through?"

"No, but of course we're not on the main trail,"

Mrs. Lewis said. "There was a rider stopped in for a cup of coffee talking about a couple men killed in Abilene." Her eyes were fixed on Sam. "Said the Irish had collected up a bounty on the pair that did it."

"Abilene?" Thomas murmured.

"I'm glad we wasn't there," Sam said. "We don't hold with killin' anything."

"Likely you carry those six-guns for ornaments," Mrs. Lewis said dryly.

"Well, I might shoot somebody trying to shoot me," Sam said seriously, "but I wouldn't ever just shoot somebody for fun."

"I wouldn't worry about it. They say the two men broke jail and headed back to Texas."

"That's just where they belong." Sam nodded, trying to hide his relief.

"Why would they do such a dumb thing as that?" Thomas objected, until Sam's boot tagged him in the leg.

"That's where the outlaws live, son," Sam said. "They always been there and always will be, likely."

"But you—" Again Sam's boot hit home and Thomas winced. "—you . . . uh . . . are always right."

"Thank you kindly, ma'am," Sam said, paying the bill and adding on some extra. "I'm not sure my horse will be too pleased with me after such a feast, but I'm completely beholden to you."

"Next time stay longer, cowboy." Mrs. Lewis looked at him intensely for an instant.

"We sure will, Mrs. Lewis," Sam said.

"And . . ." She hesitated. ". . . there was this key, hanging over the young man's saddle horn, and I thought I'd keep it safely for him." She handed over the iron ring with the jail key hanging from it.

120

PARADISE VALLEY

"Yes, ma'am, thank you ever so much," Thomas said.

"There's a tag on it." Mrs. Lewis smiled. "Abilene Jail, I think it says. 'Course my eyes are not quite so sharp as they used to be."

"Likely it's something like that, maybe its Hanni-bal, Missouri, or Helena, Montana, I don't remember just where I picked that key up," Thomas stammered.

"Thanks again, ma'am." Sam shook his head, went out the front door and down the steps to the horses.

"You collect keys?" Sam asked.

"No, Sam," Thomas said weakly.

"Then maybe you can lose it." Sam nodded, and swung aboard the big steel-dust. "I reckon our only hope is to try for Fort Hays."

"What's there?"

"I guess it's about seventy-five miles outside the knowledge of God," Sam said and kicked the big steel-dust into an easy gallop.

One mile was like the last one and the one to come, a nearly level pastureland which seemed never to end. Were it not for the ruts of past wagon trains, they would have needed a binnacle mounted on the floor of the buggy, and a constant reading of the compass.

If the wind was blowing the other way, Ruth thought tiredly, they could put up a sail and just go free all the way to the Rockies. As it was, the wind was a threnody whining over the grass, its melancholy harping never ceasing.

There were no cattle, only a few buffalo, and she fretted that she hadn't a rifle because there were still hostiles roaming the big pasture. It was one thing her father had drilled into her before she stood as tall as the Spencer, don't go anywhere without it and know

121

how to keep it clean and use it. He had taught her to shoot when she was six, and by the time she was seven she could steady down and hit a prairie dog at three hundred yards.

But now she had no weapon except her bowie knife, hardly a match for half a dozen armed Comanche.

Still, after the Battle of Bloody Stones, the Comanche had moved north, filling in the space left by the departing Cheyenne.

"Someday this whole area will be one big ranch," Raven said to pass the time and hopefully to look wise as a treefull of owls.

"I hope so," she said. "I hope they never plow it."

"Farmers won't touch it because they can't grow anything on it. Never rains much out this far."

"But it grows the grass."

"Yes, but not corn. Nobody would be dumb enough to plow up the grass. Obviously that's what grows best."

"I guess you're right," she said, uncaring. "Will we spend the night in Fort Hays?"

"No, it's shorter to cut across. We can make up a camp on some little stream along the way," he said smoothly, feeling the desire rise in him again. He could hardly contain himself, and he reached for her shoulder.

"I think I'll just hop out for a walk," she said, and before he could say no, she was striding along beside the buggy.

"Confound it, girl!" he exploded, "we can't get anywhere if you slow us down like this."

"I walk fast," she said serenely, her pace faster than the horses,' so that she came even with them in a minute and took the cheek strap of the nearest gelding as if she were leading them on.

"Honest to Pete!" he grumbled.

"It's really quite invigorating," she called back.

"I want to put them into a trot," he said.

"Fine," she said, climbing back into the buggy, adjusting the sheath of her bowie knife to a more comfortable position.

They stopped to eat the cold lunch Grannie had prepared for them, and then pushed on.

"We'll see the Rockies a long ways out," he said.

"The sooner the better."

As the sun arced into the west, the prairie lost its sullen heat and the light turned to soft gold.

Ruth was worrying about the coming night, when Dermott would make his play, one way or another. She thought of just grabbing the remains of lunch and running off, and she thought of the knife. What else could she do against a man twice her size a hundred miles from help?

Of course she could just submit and get it over with.

"You're sittin' on a gold mine," Dolly had told her once, when she'd gone looking for Elam.

But that was long ago. Maybe it was wasted, but it was hers to waste, and if she could just get back to Paradise Valley intact, she'd give her gold mine to Sam Paterson if he wanted it.

But maybe he'd married a squaw and had a little half-breed like herself. Maybe he'd just perished and blowed away from a broken heart. Maybe he'd done the smart thing and gone to California. Still and all, she hoped he'd stayed. She prayed he was waiting for her.

"Penny for your thoughts," Raven said cheerfully.

"I was just thinking about my family," she murmured, her mind once again on the prospect of spending a whole night out here alone with the big man with the bulging eyes.

Ahead she saw a dot and thought at first it was a

123

buffalo or a couple of antelopes, but as they drew closer she saw that it was a covered wagon and a couple of oxen grazing off to one side.

"Someone to travel along with," she said with rising hopes.

"I think we'll pass on by. The horses go so much faster," he said.

Now she could see that there were two men with full beards working on the wagon. They had levered up the rear wheel and blocked up the axle with buckets and boxes.

The wheel looked lopsided as one of the men pulled it free.

"They're in trouble," she said. "We'd better stop and help."

"I have no tools and no knowledge of wagons," he objected.

"Well, you go on ahead," she said. "I'll just drop off a minute and see if I can carry a message or something."

"Chinga madre," he cursed softly, his bulging eyes hard as cold iron. "All right, five minutes, no longer."

He pulled up the team and called out, "Need any help?"

"Well, we sure need something," the smaller of the bearded men, wearing a flat black hat, said. "You got any spare axle grease?"

As the bucket of grease hung from the rear axle of the buggy in plain sight, Raven could hardly say no. It hung there so it was handy to dab into the hub where it rode the axle.

Raven sighed and put on his smile.

"Of course, help yourselves."

He needed to stir his stumps anyway. Sitting in one position all day long stiffened the joints and made the belly logy.

124

He stretched and bent his knees back and forth until he felt loose again, then he went around to where the men were working.

"Wheel all right?"

"No. The spokes are dry and have worked out of round."

The burly man with big hands muttered, "Where you folks going?"

He had little eyes hidden back inside the keg of his head, Raven noticed quickly. He'd faced enough men with eyes like that across a card table, and they were always grumpy at best and poor cheaters and not much better gunmen.

"We're aiming for Fort Hays," Raven lied. "You?"

"We're going to meet a brother in Denver," the man with the little eyes said, as his partner brushed by Raven so that the .36 caliber Colt riding high on his hip was momentarily revealed.

"Missionaries?" Raven guessed.

"Nazarenes," the smaller man nodded as Raven backed away instinctively. He never liked to have a stranger get behind his back.

"Are you a believer?" the small one asked, scratching his beard.

"Let's make camp with these men tonight," Ruth interrupted, "before it gets too dark."

She was right. The lavender haze was drifting across the western setting sun, and in a few minutes the night would bring impossible darkness.

"Certainly," the man with the little eyes said. "There's Indians about, and four is better than two in a fight."

Seeing his day's dream shattered, Raven tried to make the best of it, though without a smile.

"I want to go to bed early, so we can leave before daybreak," he said shortly, and threw their blanket rolls to the other side of the buggy. Hobbling the team, he turned them out with the oxen and said, "I'd like a light supper, Ruth."

"How come you folks travelin' alone?" the short-bearded man asked.

"We're just the advance party of a larger wagon train," Raven lied again, not liking the looks of either one of these Nazarenes.

Ruth caught the lie and then wondered if maybe Raven wasn't smarter'n she'd given him credit for.

"You folks have a religion?" the one with the little eyes asked again as he lighted a small campfire of dried grass and buffalo chips.

"Not me," Raven said coldly.

"I believe in something running things," Ruth said, "but I can't put a name to it."

"The name to it is Nazarene the prophet," the bulky man said, his little eyes shining in the firelight.

"Not too many folks believe that prophet," Raven said, "but if you do, go right ahead. It's a free country."

"But you ought to be thinking of your life after death," the small one said.

"We think heathens should be saved and brought into the temple," the heavy one said.

"If I'm a heathen"—Ruth frowned—"I don't want to join."

"You're a female," the little one said. "You don't count."

"Fine," Ruth said. "That makes it easy."

"You're meant to be bred by a Nazarene." The little one said, and suddenly Raven realized the big one had faded away from the smoldering fire.

He rolled instinctively just as a burly arm came from behind him for a choke hold.

The big hand missed his throat but had Raven's

coat and jerked him away from the buggy wheel down onto the grass.

"Heathens must die," the little one said conversationally, "so that the prophet can bring the truth."

"It's not my truth!" Ruth screamed, and as she leaped to her feet to go to the aid of Raven, she found herself looking down the big barrel of a single-tube ten-gauge shotgun.

"Don't move, girl. You look like too good a breeder to hurt."

"You mean you'd kill me even after I tried to help you?" she asked, dumbfounded.

"I'll marry you, of course."

"Of course, I'm honored," she said, digging her bootheels into the turf and leaping sidewise into the darkness.

The shotgun roared, spouting flame and rocks, horseshoe nails, and lead balls into the space where she'd just been.

As the little zealot stood peering around and forgetting to reload, she leaped back at him from the side, the knife edge bringing a bead of blood from his scrawny, whiskery throat.

"Drop that goddamn gun," she grated.

He tossed the gun away, as Raven and the burly Nazarene rolled into the firelight, locked together, straining to gain the advantage at close quarters. She saw the metallic shine of a gun for a moment, then, as the Nazarene rammed his knee into Raven's groin, a muffled shot sounded.

She waited, holding the knife against the bug-eyed missionary's throat.

After a long moment, Raven crawled into the firelight, his breath coming hard and wheezing.

"Bastard tried a left-handed choke hold, almost fooled me."

"Is he dead?"

Raven slowly came up off his knees. "Well, if a ball blows the top of a Nazarene's head off, I guess even a Nazarene is dead as anybody else."

"It don't make a nevermind," Ruth said, "just so nobody thinks I'm their brood mare anxious to produce more of the same."

11

"You're a full day behind 'em," the short, thin-gutted missionary said. "He killed my pardner in cold blood, and she give me this gash." He pointed at the scratch on his neck with a dirty finger. "Run off my stock and left me afoot. Now is that any way to treat a man of God in this country full of hostiles?"

"Don't quite sound like my Ruthie, excepting I'm right glad she's got her bowie with her."

"She was aspittin' foam and ragin' like she was hand in hand with the devil," the Nazarene whined, wanting sympathy.

"Takes one to know one," Sam said. "Reckon we'll be rollin'."

"Wait—ain't you goin' to help me?" The skinny puke stared at them astonished.

"Last time I helped a Nazarene, he charged me for it." Sam smiled and kneed the steel-dust with Thomas abreast of him.

"What will happen to him?"

"Don't worry. It won't be bad enough." Sam leaned into the west wind.

Not far behind came a single rider, a short, stocky man wearing a brown-peaked hat with two dimples in its crown. An older man, he still sat his saddle straight up and easy, and there was the look of the bulldog about him.

He paused a moment to question the Nazarene and left before he had half-finished his sad tale.

He made up his mind that his quarry was heading for Denver. At first he'd thought they were heading on down into the south park where they could lose themselves in the rough cut-up country, but now he decided they were bound for the boom town, and he knew a shortcut through Kiowa country. Maybe it wasn't as safe as downtown Austin, or maybe it was safer, depending on how you looked at it.

Buildings were going up faster than the streets could be laid out. Broadway was the center, and after that it was catch as catch can. Titles to lots were cloudy and often settled with a six-gun instead of attorneys-at-law.

The silver came flooding from the big strike at Central and on up and down the great buttress of the Rockies. The Arapaho, Kiowa, Ute, and Cheyenne were simply overwhelmed by the great rush of a people into one place, and they moved away, giving Denver more room to grow.

There was a red brick federal building on Lincoln Street that held offices for judges, land agents, Department of Interior mining officials, a cell in the basement for holding prisoners, and a room for the U.S. Attorney's office, mainly occupied by two overworked marshals.

Over a block on Colfax Avenue stood the new Silver

Balmoral Hotel, with a small but elegant marble foyer and boasting three stories with eight rooms to the floor.

The manager wore a waistcoat and the desk clerk wore a black suit. The Negro bellboys were dressed in red uniforms with silver piping.

Behind the foyer was the dining room, and adjacent to the dining room the ballroom displayed its famous parquet floor and huge wall mirrors.

It was at the Silver Balmoral that Raven Dermott stopped the buggy and handed the reins to a stooped old black man wearing the customary red uniform, but with his shoes cut out on the sides because they were too small for his big feet.

Another younger bellhop took the bags from the back of the buggy, and Raven and Ruth stepped into the foyer.

Ruth gasped at the opulent mass of carved furniture, but Raven pretended he was accustomed to such elegance and proceeded to the desk.

"A room for two, please."

"Two rooms," Ruth put in quickly.

"Ah, yes. I've already begun to think of you as someone very close and dear to me." Raven smiled and patted her shoulder. "Someday soon, I hope, we'll have a moment together to think of our future."

"You're very kind, Mr. Dermott," she said politely, knowing, after seeing the way he'd killed the Nazarene, he was no land agent representing eastern investors, he was a rough-and-tumble frontier fighter who knew all the tricks from eye gouging to making one blow serve for two when the elbow came smashing across the jaw after the fist had connected.

The closer they got to home the more he seemed to expand in power. She had a faint fear that she might not be able to hold him off all the way, and wished she

131

had a few dollars of her own to buy a small gun. But she didn't, and he sure as hell wasn't going to loan it to her, so she'd have to depend on the bowie.

"I'll meet you in the dining room in an hour," he said as they followed the bellboy up the staircase to their second-floor rooms.

In the privacy of her room, she bathed and changed into fresh blouse and jeans.

Brushing her black hair with its blue shine, she looked in the mirror and saw a set, determined face, which, although only seventeen years old, seemed to have endured a lifetime of problems.

One more day and we're home, she thought, to cheer herself up and lighten her spirits. But will papa let me come back? He never came after me, just like he'd wrote me off for dead or worse. Might be he's hardened his heart against me for being such a damn-fool kid.

Dad, I'll make it up to you, she promised the face in the mirror. I hope you'll believe me.

Downstairs, Raven Dermott waited. His frock coat had been dusted and brushed, his boots shined. He'd put on his last clean shirt and doused himself with Lord Grey's Lotion, which was all but guaranteed to attract the damsels like skunks to a bee tree.

As she approached him from the lee side, Ruth thought he smelled like a squaw on a gut wagon, but she managed to maintain her smile nonetheless.

"Ah, my dear, how splendid you look after such a long, difficult journey."

"I hope we can leave the first thing in the morning for Paradise Valley."

"I'll try very hard to finish my business in Denver today and bow to your wishes, my dear," he said grandly, and escorted her to a table in the dining room

132

that seemed to be glowing, with an ironed white damask tablecloth, crystal decanters, cruets, and polished silver flatware.

As she saw her work-hardened hands against the pure white damask, she felt embarrassed and put them in her lap out of sight.

A tall Negro dressed in a white cotton jacket with brass buttons and white duck trousers brought them a menu that included such things as Blue Point Oysters on the half shell, Lobster Newburg, Veal Scallopini, Duck à l'Orange, Venison Rostada, Squab d'Alberge.

"I don't understand," she said awkwardly. "How can they have these things?"

"There is a lot of ice in Colorado territory." Raven Dermott smiled. "Choose whatever you like. For you, my dear, the sky's the limit."

"I'm not so hungry," she said. "Crackers and milk would suit me fine."

"Let me take care of it." Raven Dermott ordered the veal for her, the oysters for himself, and a bottle of cold Alsatian wine.

Ruth was dazzled by the array of silver and the uniformed attendants, and wondered if she could figure which fork was correct, what was in the cut-glass cruet that she should know about, what did you do with a napkin big enough to swaddle a baby?

"You were meant for the finer things in life, I can see that," Raven Dermott said softly trying to remember the travel articles he'd read in *Harper's Monthly.* "I can teach you all this and we can tour Europe together."

"Right now I just want to get home," Ruth said. "Here's to our future."

She clinked her goblet against his and tasted the wine. She tried not to show that it tasted a lot better'n she'd expected, like sweet grapes and sunshine blended together.

"It's sort of new to me, this kind of high livin' I mean," she said.

"But you can learn. I'll buy you gowns from the greatest couturiers in Paris, I'll buy you diamonds from the best Belgian diamond cutters, and we could live in Florence, Italy, where there is a world of pleasure and culture you couldn't dream of."

"You and me?" she asked, puzzled by his outburst.

"My dear Ruth," he said emotionally, "I've fallen deeply in love with you over our arduous journey, and I want you to be my wife. I will lay the world at your feet."

"Maybe we better just wait till I'm home and have a chance to talk to my dad and my brother," she said. "Not that I don't appreciate your sentiments, Mr. Dermott."

"I'd hoped we might be married in a church here before going on to Paradise Valley," he said, trying to hold on to his temper.

If she hadn't mentioned her brother, he could have banished the kid from his mind. Now his thoughts were brought back to the crude truth about life.

Now his dinner was spoiled because he had to consider his moves. He needed her, needed her hidden, remote ranch to hide out in until they forgot the problem with the Chicago board of trade. Then they could sell the ranch, take the money, and spend it on the good things of life.

Simple. But she had to go along with it first, or it would have to happen the hard way.

The murder of Bobby Campbell hardly entered his mind. No one could connect him to that killing, and the hell with it.

The thing about murder was that once it was done, it was done, and no sense worrying anymore about it. It settled the problem, once and for all. That's what was good about it. You shoot a man a little bit and next year he comes back at you. But killing erased the slate and opened the future. Nothing wrong with killing so long as it served your purpose.

If he had to kill the girl, that's the way it would go. You couldn't let yourself be sentimental amongst the high rollers.

Make a mistake over a woman, you're dead for a long time.

"Likely he'll find the fanciest place in town," Sam Paterson said as they rode down Colfax Avenue.

"Lots of money here," Thomas observed. "Maybe they could afford some fresh broccoli or brussels sprouts."

"He's spending Circle C money. Sixteen thousand dollars of it," Sam continued, trying to work a logic into his ranging thoughts.

He was puzzled that Raven Dermott aimed directly for Denver, which put him close to the ranch. To his mind, anybody who'd murdered a boy and robbed his money wouldn't want to go near his home for fear somebody'd see something haywire.

But . . . maybe they'd gone on to the ranch . . . Maybe the sonofabitch had bigger plans than just stealing the herd money. Maybe he planned to use Ruthie to his advantage, and then like a lightning strike, he suddenly saw the scheme.

"He wants to marry her, Thomas!" Sam declared. "He killed her husband, and now he means to marry her. Kill the old man, and he's got the richest ranch in the state. Now it makes some sense!"

135

"Do you think Ruth would marry such a polecat?" Thomas asked.

"She run off with the fool Stark fellow. Why wouldn't she let that bigshot, highfalutin cattle buyer pull the wool over her eyes?"

The obvious landmark was the Silver Balmoral, its three stories sticking out of the skyline like a square monument.

There was no hitch rail, only uniformed Negro attendants who seemed reluctant to take the reins of their horses.

"Maybe you better hold the horses until I see if they're here," Sam said, aggravated.

"I'm sorry sir, you may not leave your conveyances here," the tall old Negro said.

"The hell I can't," Sam said.

Sam strode into the marble foyer choked with heavy walnut chairs, settees, and marble-topped tables, and went directly to the desk clerk.

"I'm looking for a big man with a young lady."

"I'm sorry, we don't give out such information about our guests unless otherwise instructed," the clerk said with a nervous bug-eyed smile.

Sam glared down at him and slowly put his huge, rock-hard sunburned fists on the slick marble counter.

"I do believe they're in the dining room. Would you like me to inquire?"

"No, thanks," Sam said. "I'll inquire."

Taking off his sweat-stained Stetson, Sam walked quickly into the glittering room and stopped. There they were, over by the window wining and dining, smiling, maybe billing and cooing. How the hell should he know what a crossbreed heifer would do.

But for damned sure, she wasn't going to marry up with that skunk until she'd talked it over with her pa. Might be he'd have to hog-tie her and drape her over a

McClellan pack saddle to get her home, but he was bound and determined to do it one way or the other.

As for the big man in the gray frock coat, likely he'd have a .36 caliber Colt strapped under his arm or a heavy-calibered derringer in his vest pocket.

Looking at the big beefy man tipping the oysters down his gullet, Sam remembered Bobby, and a red haze crossed over his vision.

Shouldn't have killed Bobby.

Was no need to. Hit him once and rob him, but to just keep banging on his head till the bones broke meant the man liked killing better'n anything.

Setting himself, his heavy jaw rigid, his eyes afire, he bowlegged it across the gleaming floor, his right hand close to the walnut butt of the Remington.

So enraptured with the good wine, fine food, opulent service, and rich atmosphere, Raven Dermott almost missed the knocking of the bulldogger heels on the hardwood floor.

In a glance he saw the problem in its entirety. A serious problem. The big dumb cowboy had hung on and somehow managed to trail him here. One word about the boy, and the girl would be lost to him forever.

Kill him before he can talk to her.

"Sam!" Ruth recognized him before he'd reached the table, leaped to her feet, and wrapped her arms around him, preventing him from drawing the six-gun.

"I'm so glad to see you!"

"Me too, Ruth, but get away, I got to kill that bastard."

Raven Dermott wasn't waiting. Already the small Colt was in his right hand, and jamming it into Sam's throat, Raven Dermott snarled, "This is the man who stole the herd money!"

Ruth backed off in confusion.

"It ain't so, Ruthie!" Sam managed to choke out, and that was enough to send her into action. With a sweep of her hand, she threw the silver tureen of hot Consommé Diablo into Raven's face while Sam dropped to his knees. The .36 exploded, but its bullet only plunked a plaster statue of a cherub at play.

On his knees and rising, Sam grabbed Raven's legs together, and coming quickly erect, threw the big man over backward into the table full of chinaware.

The small Colt went flying, and Sam came close to Raven, swinging a massive right hand to his jaw that sent him skidding across the table and crashing into the next one, which had just been hastily vacated by diners who understood that when a gun goes off the best place to be is elsewhere.

As Sam dived after him, Raven dodged aside and smashed a walnut chair down on Sam's shoulders, then reached for another.

Before Raven could swing another chair, Sam kicked him hard in the kneecap, bringing him down to one knee, where he rolled aside and clambered up again, the damaged knee barely holding his weight. Before Sam could get set, Raven dived at him, wrapping his arms around his midriff, setting his teeth in Sam's ear. Sam wanted to scream in pain, but he brought both hands up and, cupping them, smashed them against Raven's ears with such force Raven lost his bite, but he came back with a jolting left hook low and a crossing right and the elbow to Sam's jaw.

Sam shook his head dizzily. He felt like throwing up. The hell with it. He spit out a gob of the extra saliva running in his mouth and delivered his own haymaker right hand, which sent Raven staggering against the wall. As Sam went after him, Raven grabbed a heavy water carafe and swung it at Sam's head, missed, and the heavy glass bottle came down near the collarbone, paralyzing Sam's left arm.

Stepping in close, Sam hit Raven in the belly twice with the good right then moved upstairs delivering swift blows until he brought down a crushing overhand right that dropped the big man to the floor like a coldcocked bull.

"You bastard," Sam said. "I'm going to kill you so slow you'll start with a scream and end with a squeak, and I'm going to enjoy my leisure time listening.

"First I'm going to slice you into strips and pour salt all over. Then I'm going to light a fire, and start with your feet.

"And after I got you rounded off, hear me! I'm going to give you to the fire ants."

"Likely a good enough idea," a familiar voice rasped, "but it ain't going to happen. He's mine."

Sam, tottering on weak legs and heaving for breath, looked up to see the man in the brown hat and marshal's badge facing him over a leveled Colt .45.

"This ain't none of your affair."

"What's he done?" Ruthie asked, coming in between Sam and the marshal.

"I've got a warrant alleging embezzlement of funds from the Chicago Board of Trade."

"More than that, he killed Bobby and robbed him of the herd money," Sam said, as gently as he could.

"It's not true!" Raven yelled, getting to his knees. "Maybe I made a little bookkeeping mistake, but nothing more than that."

"Can you prove that charge, cowboy?" the marshal asked.

"The boy was to give him the money. The boy was found dead, the money gone, and this rotten sonofabitch gone too."

"But that's not conclusive enough," the marshal

rasped. "I'll inform the sheriff down in San Antone, and if he's got some charges of murder that will stick, I'll see he swings."

"He's mine, marshal. He ain't lawyer bait. He ain't penitentiary bound for a few years. I mean to peel him and salt him and feed him to the ants."

"He's my prisoner. You give me any trouble, I'll put out your lights," the bulldoggy marshal rasped. "You understand?"

"I understand you're on the side of a killer," Sam said, "and I promise you if he don't swing, I'm coming after the both of you."

"Steady on, Sam," came the quiet, calming voice of Thomas Lamb. "Let the law handle it."

"Bobby's dead." The bad news finally sank into Ruth's unwilling consciousness, and she felt the world grow hazy.

In a second, the marshal had clamped handcuffs on Dermott's wrists behind his back and marched him out into the street.

Sam shook his head dully. His teeth ached, his left arm dangled useless, a sickness twisted in his groin, and blood dripped from his ear, yet for all that, he'd lost his man. Had him cold, but lost him. Once in a cell, they'd ship him back to Chicago where no one would know what an evil man he was and a windy lawyer would see that the judge slapped his wrist, told him to be a good boy, and sent him out to kill another harmless youngster.

It was too big a lump of gristle to swallow for him. He'd set his heart on putting that dastardly devil down, and he hadn't done it. He'd let down Bobby, and his pa, and Ruthie.

"It's over," Thomas Lamb said, patting Sam on the shoulder. "You did your best, and the law is the law. He'll pay."

"You goddamned right he'll pay. I'm going to be in that courtroom and make sure of it," Sam declared. "That's a promise."

"Oh, poor Bobby," Ruth murmured, her face in her hands, weeping silently. "Poor little Bobby."

Her cry broke into the red anger burning in Sam's mind and touched his heart. Blinking his eyes and shaking his head, trying to clear his thoughts, he put his big paw on her shoulder. "I'm so sorry, Ruth."

"Where is . . . he?"

"He's in the cemetery in San Antone. I give him a good funeral with a hired preacher and a lady to sing a hymn, and that's all I could do."

"Thanks Sam, but . . ." she stopped her thought.

"Don't say it, Ruth. I don't want that between us," Sam said alertly. "Nobody would have played it any different."

"It's no time to talk and think bad thoughts. I just want to get home to Dad, if he wants me."

"I reckon he wants you about as much as a goose wants water." Sam smiled.

Thomas coughed politely into his hand and said, "I beg your pardon, madame—or miss, whichever the case may be . . ." Then he suddenly blushed and stammered and lost his voice.

"This here is Thomas Lamb," Sam said. "Saved my life once or twice. I lost count."

"Pleased to meet you, Thomas." She shook his hand. "I'm not going to stay here any longer. Can we go, Sam?"

"Soon as we can find you a horse," Sam said, leading her out the front door.

"Just a moment, sir." The manager came forward. "There's a matter of damages. It's a rather steep bill."

"Just send the bill to the gentleman over at the federal jail," Sam said.

141

"I'm not quite sure that's sufficient," the manager said loftily.

"Fetch your bag, Ruthie," Sam said, and glaring at the manager picked up a tall Chinese vase from a carved side table.

"Why don't you add this on to Dermott's bill?"

He heaved the vase at a plaster nymph, her erotic breasts seemingly covered by a wisp of gauze. The urn and the nymph smashed together, and both fell into rubble.

"Now then, let's see how steep this bill can be," Sam grated angrily, and picking up a pint bottle of red ink from the desk, uncorked it and poured it over the snotty bastard's head.

12

With little difficulty, Sam retrieved the matched pair of Morgans and found a saddle and bridle for one of them. Putting a halter on the other, the three riders left Denver and headed for the north park.

"It's the best part of the big pasture," Thomas remarked as they rode over the rich grassland, fording the many clear streams pouring out of the Rockies. "I wonder if I might buy a few acres hereabouts?"

"How many acres do you want, Thomas?" Ruth asked.

"Oh, four or five," Thomas said. "No point in being piggy about it."

"I doubt if you can buy four or five acres anywhere around here," Ruth smiled. "Why not say four or five hundred? They'll be the same price."

"But what would I do with so much land?" Thomas asked. "Don't you know smaller is better?"

"Not in America," Sam said.

"How's Pa?" Ruth asked.

143

Jack Curtis

"Rheumatiz and ager got him down some," Sam said.

"I say, the inner bark of young willow sprouts is just the thing for clearing up rheumatism," Thomas said. "I dare say there are other herbs hereabouts which will help too."

Something untraceable but certainly real stirred in Ruth's bloodstream. Much as scientists can know an invisible star is out in the heavens by the behavior of other stars, this force slipped into the nervous system's serum or synapses, however mysteriously it worked, and altered Ruth's vision.

Here was big adoring Sam on one side of her and there was the tall proper Englishman on the other.

What genetic wickedness emerges when there are three instead of two!

Ruth was not a teaser or a cheater, yet somehow she couldn't quite control the throaty warmth in her voice as she spoke to Thomas or the detachment in her voice when she addressed Sam.

Sam felt it instantly. He'd observed the manners of heifers and fillies for most of his life, and he caught the mischievous eyes, the change in posture, the altered voice.

Dropping back, he let the pair ride ahead while he sang softly:

"Roll on you,
little dogies,
roll on you slow,
For the Firey and the Snuffy are a rarin'
to go . . ."

He observed the pair riding leg to leg, and smiled as he saw Thomas trying to keep off to the left, and yet the black Morgan somehow stayed close.

144

"We'll be going due west pretty soon," he muttered, and leading the other Morgan, kicked the steeldust into the lead and returned to the proper trail.

"What's got into you, Sam?" Ruth said, a note of reproval in her voice.

"I'm figuring on Paradise Valley, not Pike's peak," he said over his shoulder.

Shucks, he thought as he put the steel-dust into a long lope. She never learned nothing.

Lodged in the basement cell of the federal building, Raven Dermott hardly paused to contemplate his sins.

Once he'd cleaned the blood off his face, and saw that the bruises were far from permanent, he set his mind on liberty.

Torn between his fanatical craving for revenge against Sam Paterson and the girl, not to mention the English kid, and the remembrance of soft days in Matamoras and points south, where there were plenty of excellent rums and an abundance of chiquitas, he worked it out so that he could have both. It was a special kind of liberty he wanted.

He would not be free to ride to Mexico until he'd settled with Sam Paterson and Ruth Campbell.

Both would have to be dead.

But once they were gutted out of his pride, he could be free as an eagle flying above the mice and snakes and worms in the world.

His cellmate, a 'tame,' pockmarked Cherokee Indian, waiting trial for stealing cattle, a federal offense, had little to say.

"I was drunk, and they looked like mavericks to me."

"You better think up a better story than that,"

Raven Dermott said, "or you'll be breaking rocks in Leavenworth for the rest of your life."

"They caught me with the steers," the fat Cherokee said. "They would've hung me right then if there'd been a tree close."

"Tell 'em you were just riding down the trail and the damned cattle come stampeding at you from nowhere. Tell 'em you want damages from whoever owned them crazy cattle that horned your horse and caused you all this trouble."

"They was watching me for an hour, saw me cut out the twenty and drive 'em off." The Indian chuckled. "Pretty good joke on me. I made it three times, but the fourth time, they was waiting for me."

"What the hell did you think would happen? Think they'd keep on pushing cows under your nose?"

"I don't think, I drink." The Indian sighed.

After that, there was nothing much else to say. Raven Dermott held the Cherokee in such contempt he stayed on his side of the cell and paced back and forth like a timber wolf in a cage.

There must be some way to break through that door.

On the trail into the north park, the threesome rode in such a way they seemed to be all of a group, with Sam pointing the way and the other two following in tandem, but beneath that serenity, Sam's face reflected a kind of fatalistic acceptance of a destiny he hadn't chosen and didn't want. The girl was apparently unaware of the conflict her capricious presence had set in motion.

On the face of Thomas Lamb was a puzzlement. He suddenly felt alienated from Sam and fearful of the girl's mindless design.

It wasn't that she wanted him for life as a husband,

146

it was only a girlish curiosity about a type of man she hadn't encountered before. And it was in her genes, as it was in every female God ever made, to explore the possibilities of mating, to assess and weigh this advantage over that disadvantage until the sum read a plus instead of a minus. A billion years of this sort of genetic assessment and selection had brought the race this far, and great philosophers were even now heatedly engaged in powerful rhetoric saying more or less that modern man had come a long way from the cavemen.

Others were saying none of it was true. That Adam and Eve were created in the Garden of Eden as perfect people and that was that. To say to the contrary might mean eviction from the clan, stoning, or evisceration.

There would never be an end to it: was love spiritual or physical? Was it of the heart or of the glands?

That a seventeen-year-old virgin raised on the frontier could become a part of this curious repetition only made it the more strange. She knew hardly anything about other women, their wiles and contrived methods of flirtation. She had in fact been raised almost exclusively with men by men, none of them dowdy or effeminate until she met Elam Stark.

Yet somehow the throaty voice, the husky laugh, the sidewise look of the eyes, the pouting of the lip, the swelling of the breasts, had leapfrogged over her early training and brought forth another charming maiden seeking a matchup of qualities that would produce equal if not better progeny.

Sam couldn't explain it. He knew what is was well enough, but he hadn't the words either of the Bible or the naturalist philosophers' tomes to explain it.

He did know that she would end up doing whatever her blood told her to do. Still, it was more complicated, because she was half Arapaho, a completely different heritage coursing in her veins, perhaps contrary to the blood of her father.

For sure, she was spunky and some snorty whenever an ordinary cowboy came along to try gentling her down.

A freeloader bot grub in a shiny derby hat could just make her jump up and down with joy, but the plain old cowboy with bullshit on his boots didn't hardly stand a chance. Now it was the Englishman's turn. Would she break down for him like a mare at the snorting post? If she did, so be it.

Toward dusk they came to a small, clear running stream and made camp. Here there were pine trees and plenty of fuel. Even so, they kept their fire small and tucked down in the glade out of sight. There were still small bands of Kiowa and Comanche on the loose, hunting horses and guns.

Supper was simple: cornbread, beans, and smoked sowbelly. Thomas Lamb hunted through the weeds and brought back a large bunch of lamb's-quarters, which he washed in the creek, chopped up in a bowl, and, after adding salt and pepper, offered to Sam, who tasted a leaf thoughtfully but put none on his plate.

"That's goosefoot," Ruth said. "That's for horses and cows."

"It's Chenopodiaceae." Thomas smiled. "It goes by a lot of names and is very rich in calcium. I find it quite tasty."

"Maybe a little woolly," Sam said.

"It's simply delicious!" exclaimed Ruth, extending her plate for a refill. Other than a slight squinching of his eyes, Sam rode it through. Maybe it wasn't the happiest supper he'd ever had, but at least they were all together, safe and well, and in this hard world that was something to be grateful for.

"Don't you think the greens are just delicious, Sam?" She burbled on like a brook in the spring. "Have some more."

"Reckon I'm paunched out," Sam said.

"Oh, you're just sullin'," she said. "Pass him the greens, Thomas."

"No, thanks, Thomas," Sam said.

"Whatever's the matter with you, Sam? Don't you appreciate new ideas?"

"My nature, I reckon," he said levelly, holding on to his temper.

"You sound just like all the rest of the cowboys. Beans and bacon, that's it. If it isn't beans and bacon, its beans and beef."

"I ain't been down for quite a spell," Sam said.

"But what about the future? Your body needs calcium, doesn't it, Thomas?"

"Yes, everyone needs calcium as well as other things too," Thomas fretted. He wasn't sure what was expected of him and he disliked confusion. "Actually beans are very nutritious. I suppose one could survive quite well on beans and corn."

"Reckon I'll bed down," Sam said, moving away from the firelight. "I'm feeling the effects of starvation comin' on."

"You needn't be so nasty," Ruth said smartly, before she could hold her tongue.

"Likely it's due to a shortage of calcium, ma'am." He coughed and spoke in a weak voice. "Or else I got some liver flukes from eatin' greens that sheep been through lately."

Girl's got a itch she can't scratch, he thought as he slipped off to sleep.

"Are you really an English lord?" Ruth asked Thomas, once they were alone.

"No, afraid not. My father is, and my older brother will be, but second sons must go out in the world as commoners."

"Well, you must have some kind of a highfalutin kind of a title."

"I won a blue ribbon for my rutabagas at the Bedlington Competition." He smiled. "And I daresay I might be called a Knight of the Lower Garter."

"See there," she murmured, "I knew you were a knight the first time I saw you."

"Well, I daresay that's a trifle overstrong," Thomas replied modestly.

"The truth is you're just a few places away from being the king of England, isn't that right?" she said enthusiastically.

"Well, not to put too fine a point on it, I suppose a plague might make such a thing possible."

"Imagine!" she said starry-eyed. "The woman you married would be a queen."

Thomas felt a pleasant warmth talking to the girl, but he somehow felt that he was being manipulated into a position not to his liking. After all, Sam was his friend, indeed closer to him than his brother or father had ever been, and he had no desire to lose that friendship.

In the morning, Ruth was all the more the skylark.

"Oh, happy day!" she cried out to the rising sun, "we're going home!"

"Up with me! Up with me into the clouds!

For thy song, lark, is strong . . ." Thomas quoted for fun.

"Been a long ride," Sam said.

Breakfast was beans and bacon again with the remainder of last night's corn bread.

"No poke salad for breakfast?" Sam smiled at Thomas.

"No, Sam, it occurred to me last night that there was a sheep taste to the goosefoot, and certainly we wouldn't want their beastly liver flukes."

"Reckon not," Sam said.

"Yet you let us eat those greens last night without saying anything," Ruth snapped, losing her good humor.

"I recollect I mentioned they tasted woolly. After that, I figure cussin' the camp cook is as risky as brandin' a mule on the butt."

"But you held back on telling everything, didn't you?"

"Ma'am, dear little Ruthie, please, it's me, good old Sam you're talkin' to," he said softly.

"Sure, and you held back just to show up Thomas."

"Seems like I'm twixt a rock and a hard place. Damned if I do, and damned if I don't. I just don't rightly know what to tell you, girl."

"Don't call me girl!" she cried out in a fury. "You're always treating me like a drip-nosed kid, but you don't know beans from bear shit about women."

"Likely," Sam said, straight-faced.

"Oh you! You're impossible!" she howled, and turned to Thomas, who was trying to look busy saddling his horse.

"At least there's someone in the world who appreciates the beauty of nature," she said.

"Now, Ruthie, that's hardly fair to Sam."

"Sam's a good-enough cowhand if there's somebody to tell him what to do," she said, "but I'm talking about understanding."

"I'm sure Sam understands the natural world as well as I," Thomas stammered.

"Why are you standing up for him all the time? Why don't you speak for yourself?" she asked, her eyes soft and moist.

"But Ruthie, Sam has first call."

"What the hell are you talking about!" she snorted, her temper riding high again. "What do you think I am, a mare in the remuda, waiting my turn?"

"No, my dear, but I'm sure he's quite in love with you."

"He has no sensitivity," she said. "What does he know about Florence, Italy?"

"He's a man of great sensibility."

"No need holdin' up my end of the whiffle tree," Sam said. "Let's ride."

"I'm not finished," she snapped at him like a small dog at an inquisitive hound. "What do you think about . . . us?"

"Us?" Thomas murmured.

"You and me, Thomas, riding in the royal procession. The queen nodding at us."

"And then you kiss her foot," Sam said. "Don't be more foolish. Your pa is waitin' "

"Not just yet, mister, you're not runnin' my life!" she burst out. "Why couldn't we be sippin' tea with the queen if we wanted?"

"Well, I daresay there's a problem."

"What problem? Because I'm a half-breed?"

"Oh no, not at all. People of all races in the empire are welcome in the queen's chambers."

"Then what?"

"It's, as the English put it, the queen might think you're 'damaged goods' "

"Damaged goods!" She seemed to leap straight up like a frog after an overhead fly, her face flushed with anger and her eyes bright with fury. "What the hell you mean, damaged goods?"

Sam turned to recheck his cinch, his stirrups, his saddlebags, the stamped flower on his saddle, the steel-dust's mane, maybe a fly on his hoof.

"I'm sorry, it's just an expression. Not that I personally care, it's just the custom of the aristocracy to look down upon unfortunate women."

"You . . . you prude!"

"No, please don't be angry. You're quite a fine and sweet person, and I hold nothing at all from your past against you."

"I don't believe you!" She set her jaw and glared at him. "It just happens, although it's none of your damned business, that I'm still a virgin, because I want to be that way. I am not damaged, sullied, or cheapened by anything you might say."

"Please," Thomas pleaded. "I believe you. You're a darling girl."

"Then what's the matter with me?" she cried out. "I'm a half-breed squaw, all right, but I can bake a cake good enough for the king of Norway."

"Steady down, child," Sam said.

"Honestly, my dear, Sam is the man for you," Thomas said in confusion.

"No," Sam said. "She's yours. I'm giving her away."

"Sam, I can't do such a thing to a friend who has seen me through so many bad times."

"The other way, old friend," Sam said. "You saved my life down there in the quicksand and came up with some pretty bright ideas since then. No, I owe you, and I'm payin' up."

"Sam—" Thomas stammered nervously, "she's yours. You're meant for each other."

"Something you're not telling me?" Sam guessed.

"Only that I want the best for you."

"You got another girl somewhere." Sam smiled.

"Ah, that's it!" Ruthie cried out. "Well, you don't need to be giving me back and forth, I can just goddamned well take care of myself, and I got the say-so on who I give what to."

"Where is she?" Sam ignored Ruthie's remonstration and smiled at the shy Englishman.

"Well, actually Sam, she's in England . . ."

"Engaged?"

"To tell the truth, Sam, yes," Thomas managed to choke out.

"Of course," Sam said. "I should have guessed."

"Engaged! Well, why the hell didn't you say so!" Ruth stormed.

"I was rather hoping someone would ask," Thomas said meekly.

"I suppose she's real pretty and wears Belgian diamonds and French gowns, and drinks her tea with one finger," Ruthie snarled.

"Well, she's a bit nearsighted, I daresay, needs spectacles, you know, and has a bit of a problem with too many teeth. It's the inbreeding, you know. Have to get her weight down too. But she is definitely a lady. Has a degree from the Horticultural Institute at Cambridge."

"And children?" Ruth asked, calming down.

"We'll hold off . . ."

She stared at him as if he was as out of place as a cow on the front porch. Then she shrugged and repeated, "Hold off?"

Then she laughed. "Hold off!" she hooted. "Honest to God, Thomas, I'll bet you couldn't teach a settin' hen to cluck!"

"Steady on," Sam said.

"You just shut your pan and sing dumb, Sam, or I'll wool the sparks outta you," she growled, mocking herself, and with a grin mounted the black Morgan.

"Yes, ma'am," Sam said, not daring to smile, but feeling a bounteous joy in his heart.

"Reckon you better lead the way," Sam said.

"No, Sam, I'm on to you. It's your play, high-low-jack and the game."

"Likely we been too serious from all the hardness of the trail," Sam said, chucking the crestfallen Thomas on the shoulder. "Speakin' for myself, I'll like to meet your lady and show her around the spread."

"Count me in on that, too," Ruth said firmly. "By the way, what's her name?"

"Oswaldine," Thomas Lamb murmured miserably.

"Don't be so downhearted." Sam laughed. "Hell, maybe the boat'll spring a leak and turn back!"

"Oh noble Sam." Thomas smiled. "You're so good at bringing things back to an even keel."

"Thomas, out here you got to learn to never interfere with nothing what don't bother you none."

That morning, which brought only the faintest light from an airshaft into the basement cell, Raven Dermott was going crazy. He couldn't stand the cage. He was beginning to worry about a flood or an earthquake or a fire. Anything just a little bit out of kilter in nature could come down on him and kill him without mercy. His eyes were sunken and his mouth trembled.

"Best settle down," the Cherokee said. "You just wearing out your boots for nothing."

"I've got to get out of here," Raven said. "I've got to get some air."

"They goin' hang you." The half-breed chuckled. "Ain't no air when that happens."

"They don't hang me. They don't cage me," Raven raged. "I'm bigger than them and I'm a hundred times smarter."

"Sure, sure, mister." The Indian smiled. "Only they're out there and you're in here."

155

"I need a surprise. Something to make them forget the routine."

"They ain't ever going to open that door," the Indian said, "unless there's four of 'em with scatter guns. They shove your grub through the bars and you pass it out secondhand the next day."

"You think you're funny?" Raven screamed. "Shut up, you fool!"

"Settle down, or they'll pack you into a round cell padded with leather."

"That's for loonies," Raven yelled. "Goddamn it, I'm not crazy! I've done nothing wrong. I made a small error in bookkeeping, nothing else!"

"When do you go to trial?"

"How do I know? They haven't even found an attorney for me."

"Likely they expect you to plead guilty and save some time."

"Whose time? My time is valuable!" Raven Dermott raged on. "The goddamned fools! I could have made a million dollars since I been sitting in here as an innocent man."

"I've heard that before," the Indian said, grinning.

"What would be something they wouldn't expect?" Raven Dermott said, thinking aloud. "Something that would shock even the jailers? Something that would make them come in and forget all about me?"

Eyes blazing like a mad zealot, he stared at the lumpish Cherokee. "What would bring them in here and turn their backs?"

"Hell, I dunno. Nothing I can think of."

"I can think of something," Raven grated, seeing the whole thing in his mind and how to stage it to make it work.

A desperate chance, yes, but at least a chance!

Turning away, he unbuckled his narrow calfskin

belt and pulled it free from his trouser loops. Rolling it into a coil he could conceal in one hand, he turned slowly and said, "Is there anything in that air shaft?"

"What do you mean?"

"I thought I saw a bird. A bird like a robin fly down there."

The Indian turned to look up at the small dim window.

"Couldn't be . . ." he said, just before Raven whipped the belt over his head and jerked it tight around his throat.

With his height and weight he had no trouble strangling the Indian once he had the belt gripped around his neck.

When he felt the body jerk spasmodically and twitch in the final throes of death, he climbed up on the bunk and hoisted the body against the back wall, where he could secure the end of the belt around an iron bar, leaving the body to droop and dangle, the face black with congested blood, eyes bulging, tongue protruding.

Satisfied, he pulled a blanket off the bunk, lay down in the dark corner next to the door, and commenced howling like a gut-gored mule. "Hooooooweeee-ooooooh!"

"Hoooooweeeeooooooh!"

A guard came to investigate. "Hey, what the hell . . .?"

And seeing the hanging carcass said, "Holy Christ!" and ran back up the stairs.

In a moment, four guards carrying shotguns came running down, and seeing the hanging horror, opened the door and pushed in, forgetting in that one instant that Raven Dermott was somewhere inside, even as a crumpled shadow in the dark corner.

As soon as the last one was in, mad-eyed Raven

Dermott leaped from his blanket, cracked the last guard's neck with a ferocious rabbit punch, seized the double-barreled shotgun, and backed into the hall.

Slamming the door and locking it swiftly before they even knew he was loose, he yelled, "Hold it there, break those guns or I'll burn you down!"

The three guards whirled and stared at the big man eyeing them over the two barrels loaded with double-ought buck.

"You can't get out," the captain said.

"I'm out. Break those guns. Right now!"

The three men slowly flipped the thumb levers, the shotguns swung open, and the brass hand-loaded shells popped out onto the floor.

"Now. Face the wall on your knees. Be quick!"

As they complied, Raven ran up the stairs two at a time, but on reaching the main-floor level, he stopped a moment to compose himself.

He probably looked like a desperado, yet he had to pass through the main floor looking harmless. He couldn't give up the shotgun, but to show it would give him away.

Quickly stuffing it down his right pants' leg, he held the butt with his hand in his pocket and bent over like a hunchbacked cripple. His head down, lank hair dangling, he commenced to crab down the broad hall. At the door were two officers facing the street, checking people coming in.

Limping and scraping, Raven saw a side door that was unguarded, and showing only his bowed back and a rigid right leg, he made his way to it, opened the door, and crabbed outside only half observed by the officers, whose first inclination was to think that he was a war veteran looking for the pension office.

Half a block down Lincoln Avenue, Raven Dermott stepped into a dark doorway, pulled the shotgun out of his pants' leg, and carrying it lightly in his right hand like a man going to a gunsmith, he went out into the street again, his lowered eyes busy looking for the best horse in the block.

Hurry! his mind screamed. Those guards would be giving the alarm at any second!

Ah, let them, he thought as he saw a big chestnut thoroughbred at the hitch rail.

Leaning against the rail, he unobtrusively undid the hitch and waited until there was a howl from the Federal Building.

As the citizens along the block turned to look that way, he mounted the chestnut and turned the other way, going at an unobtrusive trot.

Turning the corner and out of sight, he kicked the long-legged gelding in the flanks and sent him flying north up Federal Boulevard.

In three minutes he was well clear of town and out in the wide-open frontier, riding a fine strong horse and carrying a loaded double-barreled shotgun.

They'd never catch him on the thoroughbred.

The trail to north park, where he knew he could find Paradise Valley, was well used at first, and he set the chestnut going at a long lope that ate up the miles, yet appearing so easy and natural to the wagons and riders he passed they took little note of him except to envy his mount.

In an hour, he let the chestnut walk and gather breath, and he noticed the trail was less and less worn, as if it would soon peter out.

He'd have to watch it. Pretty soon it would fork five ways, or just phase out into a little flat and disappear.

Still, he was sure that the three of them were ahead of him, that three horses would leave tracks.

The posse would be confused, they couldn't know he was riding the chestnut until its owner reported it. That might be a minute or half a day. With any luck, then, it would be at least an hour, and if he had an hour's head start, they'd never find him.

Any escaping criminal would naturally ride south, the going was easier and the border beckoning.

His confidence returned as he reviewed the way the thing had worked out. He'd operated on instinct alone, but now, as he considered his moves, he thought he'd been right every time.

The Mormon Trail was just a short ways north, and he'd cross the mountains on it after he'd wiped out that nest of proud snakes.

As he rode along, he considered another option. Suppose after he killed the big cowboy, the Englishman, and the girl's old man, suppose he locked her up somewhere until she saw the error of her ways.

No. Better to sluice the whole tribe and go right on over to Salt Lake, then on to Sacramento, where he'd blend in with the politicians.

Call me governor Raven Dermott, friend of the people, he teased himself, and laughed. It wasn't as farfetched as it sounded.

He could challenge a couple of the mucky-muck politicians to duels and clear the way. Watch 'em scatter.

Big money and no punishment even if you're caught with your hand in the money box.

Politics. The more he thought about it the more he liked it.

The old shell game. He knew it well. You line up

with the rich and give your promises to the voters. Everybody gets just what they deserve.

He envisioned himself wrapped in Old Glory, standing on a platform, a halo around his heavy black curls, leading the audience in "America the Beautiful."

It's a natural, he thought. It's me.

PARADISE VALLEY

13

Paradise Valley was a long wild grass meadow straddling ten miles of Paradise Creek, a cold, tumbling stream full of rainbow trout, protected from the rawest of storms by rising mountains timbered with spruce and pine. From the Circle C ranch house, at the upper end, you could look down the meadow divided by a ribbon of brush and timber along the creek and count your cattle crop with a spyglass.

The creek issued from the base of a high granite cliff that cut off the rise of the valley, making the only possible entrance the lower end, which ultimately expanded into the high prairie of eastern Colorado.

So it was not unusual that old Micah Campbell sat on the front veranda, taking in the morning sun from his padded chair, watching the cattle and a small herd of mule deer feeding in the deep grass.

He was expecting a herd of two thousand Texas cattle almost any day now. It seemed like a year since Bobby and Sam had ridden off.

It was supposed to be a learning trip for Bobby, who'd never been farther from home than Denver. It was good training for the boy, who would soon replace him, but who would have more trouble with federal agents and fast-talking land grabbers than he'd ever had with the Arapaho.

The fact was he didn't need the extra cattle. When they arrived, he'd have to sell two thousand fat four-year-olds. But he did need to know that Bobby could handle the parasites.

The stigma laid on half-breeds was a cheap way of making a man feel less than he was. For his part, he thought the mix of Scotch and Arapaho threw off-spring smarter and stronger than their parents. But you had to get out in the hard world to find that out. You had to learn who you could trust and who you couldn't. Sometimes it was just luck, but in the end, if you made it through, experience paid off.

For sure the outside world wouldn't let an un-trained country boy keep this valley unspoiled and free, even though it had all been proved up and done legal.

Those folks outside had ways of changing the laws to suit themselves no matter what the Constitution and the Bill of Rights said.

Off to the left the cookhouse chimney lazed out a plume of smoke as Ira Lauder, the sprung-legged cook, fixed breakfast for himself and the two ranch hands who would be riding the rimrock all day making sure the cattle didn't stray.

Sometimes the Arapaho camped at the lower end of the valley, putting up their tepees and bringing in their horse herd, and that was according to the agreement he'd made with the chief twenty years ago. Old Fire Tree was long since dead, and his son Red

Bird ran what was left of the tribe. If they had to, they killed a cull steer, but they preferred buffalo and deer to beef, and it seemed the fewer the buffalo, the fewer the Indians, so that the number of beef given to them stayed about the same.

They were always coming and going, looking for a fight with the Kiowa or the Potawatomi, stealing horses more for thrill and pride than anything else, although they were always getting killed doing it.

It wasn't in them to just settle down and take it easy, they kept wanting to prove how brave and smart they were, and he reckoned with all the new rifles and big cartridges coming in, it wouldn't be long before there wouldn't be an Arapaho or even a Kiowa left to enjoy the park.

He'd gone with them a few times when he first came into the country. They'd hit the Kiowa and sneaked off with some horses, and they'd had a big celebration to dramatize their cleverness and courage, but he couldn't see the point in it. Nothing changed. Three months later, the Kiowa sneaked in and took back their horses and a few extras. Hardly seemed to make sense to a Scotchman.

Yet they'd respected him when he said no, he wouldn't go anymore, he just wanted to raise cattle. Old Fire Tree had given him Snow Bells, his tall, clear-eyed daughter, and that made him brother to Red Bird, so there never was a question about the land or the beef.

And he had proven you didn't have to treat an Indian like a yeller dog just to make yourself stand taller.

The only thing wrong with Paradise Valley was its remoteness from the rest of the world. It was hard to keep a good cowhand on that account, and old Micah

PARADISE VALLEY

Campbell was wondering now if maybe he'd over-
reached himself in his youth and come to own a place
he couldn't live on alone anymore.

Of course, he could listen to Ira Lauder complain
about his sprung leg or lie about all the women that
chased him all the way from Canada, or he could set
with the ranch hands who never had much to say
except the grass was growing.

He reckoned he'd try to hang on another year, but if
it didn't get a little more sociable by then, he'd just sell
some cows, move to Denver, and fort up in some
backwater hotel for old-timers.

Darn that Ruthie. Just couldn't wait till his back
was turned before she started horsin' for a man. The
heck with her. If that's all she thought of him and the
valley, then let her enjoy what she wanted. He tried to
keep her out of his mind, but with Bobby gone it
wasn't so easy.

Shame on you, girl. Your momma would cut your
hair off for that trick, and if you give her any sass,
she'd cut your nose off next.

Damn the TB. Between the TB and the smallpox
and the repeating rifles, the Indians were going downhill so fast they'd never come back.

How could the good Lord allow TB to come into
Paradise Valley and take ahold of my good wife, who
wasn't even twenty-five years old yet?

Tears formed in his old hound-dog eyes as he
remembered her going, not being extra brave or extra
scared, just day by day fading away until she drowned
in her own blood and he buried her over by the blue
spruce, where sometimes he could see her standing
there with bright eyes and a merry smile.

"Been alone too long," he growled aloud, and
jerked his mind off the sadness of the past and

wondered what was spooking the deer down the valley.

His knees creaked like rusty hinges and pained him when he got up and went inside for his brass spyglass.

Bringing the glass out to the porch, he sat down again and settled it on the railing. The deer were already flushed and gone. The cattle had their heads up and were watching downstream.

What was upsetting the life in his paradise?

There had been a sewing-machine salesman two years ago in a fitted-out spring wagon, but he was lost and crazy from fear, and old Micah had sent a hand to guide him back to Denver.

Then he made out the three riders and the extra black horse. They weren't Indians. Two of 'em were big tall fellows, but the third one was just a squirt in the milk bucket, although there was something familiar about the tiny distant figure in the stained flat-crowned Stetson.

The phrase "a little piece of leather, well put together" passed through his mind. He used to call Snow Bells that in the good times, and he thought he must be dreaming or going as crazy as the sewing-machine salesman, because Snow Bells was lying over there under the blue spruce, so it couldn't be her riding up the valley.

Dang it, he complained impatiently, because his eyes were not as keen as other times when he would have been able to spot a horsefly on the hind leg of the black horse she was riding.

It couldn't be Ruthie. Could it? She'd run off with a flannelmouth in a shiny derby hat . . .

Was it?

Agitated, he got to his feet, forgetting his creaky knees, and almost dropped the telescope. Goddamn

166

it, I ain't cleaned house in three months, he thought, and I ain't changed pants in two weeks. Ain't shaved since a week of Sundays. Good Lord. They's a woman comin!

"Ira. Ira!" he yelled in a panic. "Ira, they's a woman coming."

Old Ira gimped out with the usual greasy flour sack wrapped around his middle and yelled back, "Can't hear ya."

"I say they's a woman comin!" old Micah yelled again, cupping his knotted hands to his mouth.

"Well, boil me for a seahorse," old Ira yelled back, "ain't that nice!"

"Nice! You blamed idjit, we're dirty'n calf splatter in a hencoop!"

"Fine," old Ira hooted back. "It'll keep her so busy she won't be able to talk."

Steadying the spyglass against the porch column, he sighted them in again. Now he could see it was Sam Paterson in the lead on his good steel-dust, then behind him came a tall fence rail of a man with fair skin, and behind him rode his girl Ruthie.

He studied her posture and her way of riding. She didn't look beat down or anything. Likely tired from a long ride, but still her head was up and she was tallyin' the cattle as they passed through. But where was Bobby?

Bobby must be with the cattle. He's taken charge the way he should. Bringing 'em slow so's they ain't losin' any tallow.

"Ira!" he yelled.

"Now what?"

"Ira, go down to the slaughter shed and kill that lame heifer. We're goin' to have company."

"Dag on it, I told you I done killed and butchered

167

her yesterday. The meat's hanging in the spring-house."

"That's better. Thanks, Ira," old Micah called back, remembering, and deciding to keep his mouth shut from now on or likely they'd send him to Denver strapped to his chair, with a meal sack over his head.

Far up the valley, Sam could see the outline of the ranch buildings and make out the old blue spruce off to the right of the main house. There was the bunk-house, and the stone springhouse, then the pole barn and lean-to, then off downwind was the slaughtering shed where the buzzards came circling every day, then on down a ways was a big pole corral holding half a dozen riding horses and next to it the blacksmith shop. It was all a man needed, he reflected.

Plenty of good water and grass, fuel and building material in the timber, and if a man wanted, he could put in a waterwheel for milling grain or making boots.

He should have been feeling glad to be back, but his heart was full of dread for what he had to tell old Micah. Going to have to jump the highest fence ever made, he thought, ain't no way to back off it, but how do you tell an old man you lost his only son to a coyote?

I guess he'll know by just looking at me. Maybe that'll give him a little slack, make some breathing room while the shock wears off.

They rode directly to the old log house with the veranda across the front. They dismounted and teth-ered their horses, waiting for old Micah to appear.

Ira Lauder was crouched by the cookhouse window, peeking out. It wasn't his right to welcome anybody. If old Micah stomped out and told 'em to scat, that's what would happen, and old Ira didn't want to be in the middle of that hoedown.

168

"Hello the house!" Sam Paterson called.

Suddenly old Micah charged out on the veranda, wearing a clean shirt half unbuttoned, his face marked with razor scrapes, his hair wild.

"Come on in!" he yelled. "Goldang it, what are you waiting for, Christmas?"

Ruthie looked up at him, moisture in her eyes, and she accused herself of being a sniveling female.

"Come, Ruthie, give you old pa a hug!" Micah grinned.

Ruthie leaped up the steps and into his arms. She felt his bones in her embrace and thought she'd best be putting some flesh back on him.

"Dad, I'm sorry," she choked. "I treated you badly."

"Hellsafire, don't never be sorry for something you got through. You're home! That's the main thing!"

"I'm going to do better by you, Pa," she said firmly.

Looking over her shoulder old Micah saw the tall young man hanging back, and then he saw the grimness lining Sam Paterson's weathered features.

He knew it right then, but he couldn't put a name to it.

Releasing Ruthie, he shook hands with Sam and said, "Glad to see you back, Sam. Who's this young man?"

"Thomas Lamb. He's from England."

"You're a far piece from home," old Micah said. "You're welcome here."

All the time, as he was going through the motions of being polite, he was seeing the doom on Sam's face and knew he was going to have to bite the hardest bullet he'd ever bit, and he'd tried some over the years.

When he couldn't stand it any longer and when he

thought he was ready for it, he asked Sam in a quiet voice, "Bobby?"

"I lost him. I still don't know all of it, but for sure I lost him."

Old Micah sucked air for a few seconds and asked, "An accident?"

"He wanted to pay the broker for the herd. I figured the man to be just an ordinary percentage crook. I didn't figure him for robbin' and killin'."

"Likely Bobby wanted to do it."

"Yes sir, but I didn't read the evil in that man."

"No mistake? No chance of it being different?"

"I gave him a proper burial in San Antonio. I'm sorry, he's gone."

"And the agent who robbed and killed him?"

"A man named Raven Dermott. Had a good reputation, and looked well off."

"I don't care about that, Sam," old Micah rasped. "Did you kill him or do I get to?"

"I chased him to Denver. Caught him there, but the danged U.S. marshal took him away from me. I'm going back soon as I can, in case they let him loose."

"I'll go with you," old Micah said solidly.

Again he took a minute to breathe and absorb the hard jolt. With the boy gone, his life showed up for nothing. Snow Bells's death was meaningless, his own forty years of fighting futile. If there were any Indians able to hold it, he'd give the ranch back to them, but there weren't, and he wouldn't give it to corrupt federal officials.

So it was all just like hollering down a hole, wasted time.

Was a good boy, too, a good mix of the bloods. He'd kind of wanted to see how it would firm up when the boy had a few years more, but it wasn't going to happen. Wasted. All of it. Done for nothing.

He felt the day go gray and a dizziness turn his balance, and he sagged against the porch railing.

"Pa, sit down here," Ruthie said, quickly taking him by the shoulder and guiding him to the padded chair.

"I'll be all right in a minute," he mumbled. "Just the excitement I guess. Can't handle it anymore."

She ran into the kitchen and found the bottle of Kentucky bourbon kept there at all times, poured half a glass, and returning, put it in his hand.

"What's this?" he asked, looking up at her.

"It's whiskey. It's good for what ails you."

"Where's the others? I ain't goin to celebrate your comin' home drinking by myself!"

"Oh, Pa!" She hurried back to the kitchen for the bottle and more glasses.

When each had a drink in hand, old Micah said, "I want to welcome Ruthie home, I want to thank young Thomas Lamb for helping out, and Sam for doing his best." He lifted his glass. "Here's to kindness."

Then he drank as the others repeated his traditional toast.

"Here's to kindness."

"Red and Downie are out riding the rimrock and won't be back before dark, but by golly we can have us a feast anyways," old Micah declared.

"Have you ever tried to grow cucumbers or okra here?" Thomas asked politely.

"No, the ground just grows grass," old Micah said. "We have a late frost in the spring and an early frost in the fall, sort of holds down on the gardening even though it can be very fine weather most of the time."

"What a shame," Thomas said. "I was hoping I could help out a little. I brought some seeds and things along."

"Any lily bulbs?"

"Yes, sir, I've got some purple iris."

"Do me a favor, Thomas," old Micah said, looking away. "Make a little flower garden over there by the blue spruce. I'd be much obliged to you."

Whipping the long-legged chestnut, Raven Dermott rode with the fury of a madman. By now the trail was marked only by an occasional blaze on a pine tree, but he drove the horse on without rest.

He was certain that once Sam Paterson learned he'd escaped, he'd come on his track like a bulldog, never quitting until he had his revenge.

Well, Raven Dermott was just some smarter'n that. He'd fix Mr. Paterson before he ever knew what hit him. When Raven Dermott left Colorado there would be no one on his trail, and by the time he reached California the U.S. marshals would have forgotten him.

But first he had to down Sam Paterson.

Need a good long-barreled rifle, say about a .45 caliber or bigger. Long range.

The kid had said you could see the whole spread from the front porch. So that meant you could see the front porch from anywhere. That meant he'd come in sidewise, bide his time, and make a long shot. Just one. Down goes Paterson, and Howdy-do California!!

The shotgun was devastating at short range but worthless in an ambush. Somewhere along the way he thought maybe there'd be a country store or a way-stop for travelers, but he found nothing, and he eased the thoroughbred to a walk while he tried to work out a plan. No sense in busting into that valley with the wrong gun.

Surely folks rode this trail once in a while.

Then he heard a voice ahead of him, a man singing. Kicking the chestnut into a gallop, he quickly

overhauled an old man on a white mule, leading a
heavily loaded burro.

The old man was singing a fast paced rouser:

"Old Dan Tucker's a fine old man,
Washed his face in a frying pan,
Combed his hair with a wagon wheel
Run away with a toothache in his heel . . ."

"Howdy, stranger." The old prospector grinned.
"Caught me singing to my mule, Susan Van Dusen."

"Don't stop on my account," Raven said. "Going
far?"

"A ways," the old man said, his vagueness intended.
"Mind if I ride along?"

"You can go faster by yourself," the old man said,
not quite saying he'd rather be alone.

But by then Raven Dermott had seen the iron-
trimmed walnut stock of the Springfield .45–70 sticking up from under the old man's right leg. Lifting the
short shotgun, he fired at close range before the old
miner ever had time to think of running or fighting.
The mule tried to run, but the burro tied to it didn't
want to, so it was no problem catching the both of
them and taking the Springfield.

The body of the old man fell to the earth, and
Raven reckoned he'd have no money on him because
he was going away from Denver instead of coming in.

And there would be nothing of value in the burro's
pack. Only tools and provisions. No. Get free of the
grisly scene before another stranger came by.

Throwing aside the useless greener, Raven drove
the thoroughbred on north. Surely there would be a
sign or something. All he needed now was to find the
ranch and make one shot count.

* * *

173

Jack Curtis

"I'll show you around," Sam said to Thomas, who was feeling giddy from the whiskey.

"Yes, might clear the head," Thomas agreed quickly, and went with Sam over to the cookhouse, where Sam introduced him to Ira Lauder, who was slicing thick steaks from a beef loin.

"Make yourself at home. You heard the boss yell at me. If I don't make her lickety-split, he'll turn me over to the Injuns."

"Some wild shallots might make your beef a bit more savory."

"That may be, yes, that may be," the old cook said, concentrating on his work, and willing to agree that a boar had tits if they'd just leave him alone.

"Down here is the barn." Sam guided the young Englishman on across the low slope.

"I say, I did make a beastly mess of it with Ruth."

"Not really. If you're engaged, you can't very well say otherwise."

"She's yours, Sam. She knows it and I know it."

"I reckon I'll let her spread her loop when she's ready. Likely I could be caught."

"And this?" Thomas asked, indicating the low square stone building.

"The springhouse." Sam opened the heavy plank door revealing a spring coming up through the floor and flowing on out through a hole in the wall. "Keeps things cool," Sam said, indicating the quartered beef hanging from the log rafter.

"All you need is a hot spring," Thomas smiled.

"There's one over the hill," Sam said. "Old Micah sets in there sometimes for his rheumatism."

They passed by the barn and corral and the black-smith shop, and Sam was ready to turn back.

"That old building, what's that?"

"That's the slaughterin' shed. Has the hooks and gambrel and a block and tackle for the heavy stuff. Old Ira keeps his meat saw and cleavers in there and some spices and salt and such."

"So you're really almost self-sufficient."

"We need to bring in flour and beans and such," Sam said, leading the way back to the house.

"And that big blue spruce, what's special about that?" Thomas asked.

"Micah's wife's buried there. He wants to be beside her when he goes. I wish I could have brought Bobby back. Goldarn it." A misery gaunted his face.

"Sam. It wasn't your fault. It's the way the cards were dealt out."

"They was stacked against us," Sam said grimly, "and I hate to be cheated, even by some God supposed to be running the spread from a bench upstairs."

They rambled on back to the bunkhouse, where Sam showed Thomas his cot.

"You can stay as long as you like," Sam said.

"I can't really. I think I should be traveling to Oregon soon. I've heard it's a good place for growing."

It wasn't much of a sign. Only a pine slab branded with the Circle C propped between rocks at a fork in the trail.

But it was enough.

Now Raven held the tall horse to a slow trot, his eyes searching every bush and tree in front of him. He dared not come over a little rise and find himself in an open valley.

The trail led slightly downhill. It would have to come into a large drainage, and that drainage would have to be the Paradise Valley spread.

As the timber thinned out and the trail seemed to be more traveled, he brought the thoroughbred to a walk, hoping to keep the sound of his hooves muffled in the heavy duff.

Even then, he almost popped out into the long meadow. One minute there was timber, the next minute it was wide open and full of fat beeves.

There was a fortune in cattle right before his eyes, but he wouldn't think of it until after he'd rid himself of that sticktight Sam Paterson.

Drifting back into the trees, he worked his way up the long slope's concealment.

Occasionally he'd take a turn to the left to make sure of his ground, and then after he located the ranch house farther up yonder, he felt a surge of joy that he was about to finish the whole damned business. Finish it and ride free!

He saw the horses, his matched black Morgans and Sam's steel-dust, and knew he had his man.

Dismounting, he tied the chestnut to a birch sapling and, walking in a crouch, came to a great pine log that had slowly weathered its way into a natural ambuscade.

Time had eroded most of the bark and soft wood, leaving the golden pitch-pine skeleton as hard as flint. Yellow glistening snags poked into the air like wild-cattle horns. Perfect.

He levered a brass cartridge into the chamber and carefully laid the rifle barrel between two of the sharp pitch-pine snags, making an effective screen for him as he peered over the log.

A hundred yards across the slope was the main log house. An old man was sitting with his back straight as a ramrod in a padded chair.

Sam and the Englishman were just now coming up the steps as Ruth went inside.

Now all he had to do was take a bead on the big cowboy's left breast pocket and squeeze the trigger.

"See anything strange?" old Micah asked carefully as they sat on a bench near the old man.

"No. The cattle look good. Why?"

"Quail covey flushed out a minute ago from over yonder," the old man murmured, making a slight motion with his eyes.

No one looked off that way.

Muscles tensed, Sam said to Thomas, who was in effect shielding him from that hillside, "Maybe you ought to go in and talk to Ruth, Thomas."

"No, you don't," Thomas said, sotto voce, his lips hardly moving. "No one wants to kill me. What's going on?"

"Could have been a blue fox worrying the birds," old Micah said.

"I reckon you been living with that hill for forty years, you oughta know if it was a fox or not," Sam said.

"I'd say it was not," old Micah said tightly. "I wish't I had my old buck shooter next me right now."

"I don't know of anybody wants to harm us," Sam said. "Could it be Red or Downie coming in the back way?"

"They'd sing out," old Micah said.

Ruthie came out bearing a tray full of crackers and rat cheese and passed it around before putting the tray on the table.

"Best stay inside, Ruthie," old Micah said.

She shot him a glance and saw the tightness around his eyes, then she turned to Sam and saw the same thing.

"They's a sidewinder over on the hillside," Sam said. "Soon as Thomas moves out of the way, I got a feeling there'll be some lead going by."

"I can go out the back door with my little varmint rifle," she said. "Maybe peg him down."

"Too big a chance. Might be more'n one," Sam said. "I reckon we're all going to just make a dive for that door soon as you're inside."

"Hell of a note," old Micah growled.

As Ruthie went on inside, Sam said, "Listen, Mr. Campbell, I want you in first. Then Thomas and then me. Understood?"

"I thought I was ramroddin' this spread," Micah said.

"Right now, I'm takin' charge, because I'm the one elected."

"Who elected you, Sam?" Old Micah smiled, rising and hobbling toward the door.

"I reckon I elected myself," Sam said, and as soon as Micah was safely in the door he said, "Thomas, you're next."

"You first," Thomas said. "As soon as I move, you'll be exposed."

"Let me do it my way," Sam said. "I want you in there if I have to throw you."

"Will you stand up the same time as I, Sam?"

"No. I was figuring on dropping and rolling clear," Sam said. "Now quit trying to run my show. Just act natural and scat."

Thomas gravely stood and walked slowly toward the door, trying to shield Sam as long as possible, but there came a moment when it was fish or cut bait, and the second he leaped at the door, a heavy ball came screaming across the porch, catching Sam in the shoulder as he dived to the floor.

Had a bead on me all the way, Sam thought, even while rolling down the three steps and under the hitch rail where the horses screened him.

The bitter pain in the shoulder made his eyes blur and he felt like throwing up, but he forced himself to concentrate on the bushwhacker somewhere up there in the trees.

Somehow he had to get into the edge of the timber, but it was a long run across a lot of open space.

There was another way, if he could do it.

Reaching out from behind the steel-dust, Sam loosened the quick tie and then tried to grab the saddle horn, meaning to ride in one stirrup to the trees, keeping the horse's body between him and the rifleman, but as he tried to grip the leather-wrapped horn, the pain in his shoulder stabbed deeply, and he lost his grip. The horse hadn't moved, but Sam couldn't move either.

He was ready to try grabbing the horn with his right hand and do it all backwards, without the six-gun in his hand, when he heard the report of a small rifle up on the slope, and then the boom of the big rifle.

Sam ran as hard as he could for the trees.

He'd recognized Ruthie's light Winchester, and hoped the bushwhacker had his attention concentrated on her.

He'd almost made it when a heavy four-hundred-grain bullet crashed somewhere to the right of his middle and sent him rolling. And as the bushwhacker rose to sight him in for a kill shot, another rifle boomed from the house, and the big man dropped behind the log again.

Sam didn't stop to worry about his pain or his blood. With six-gun in hand he charged the hill, crazy as a grizzly bear gone berserk.

He'd recognized the rifleman as Raven Dermott and there was nothing in God's green world that could stop Sam Paterson from taking him down.

Jack Curtis

Raven Dermott was all but pinned down by the small rifle off to his right and the big old buffalo rifle in the house. He knew Sam Paterson was coming in on his left and he decided to retreat and at the same time finish off the man he'd come for.

Slipping behind a pine tree and backing on to another he aimed to meet up with the tall thoroughbred at about the same time Paterson would break up over the slope.

Fine. There was the chestnut. Now where was Sam Paterson?

He crouched, the rifle at the ready, and waited, listening to every pine needle falling.

But there was nothing. Trembling now with fear of the silence and vast emptiness, he moved toward the thoroughbred.

Somehow the quick slipknot had come undone and the horse, smelling his fear, shied away.

Calming himself, he moved slowly toward the just-out-of-reach reins. In a minute the damned horse would step on a trailing rein and that would stop him for the second he needed.

Passing by a giant white pine, he saw the horse falter and reached for the rein. At that moment he felt the steel muzzle come up against the side of his head.

"Drop the rifle."

"Of course," he said quickly, and dropped the rifle so that it fell across the toe of his boot.

The steel barrel came away from his head and he turned enough to see the big cowboy, his left arm hanging and blood dripping off his fingers, his eyes like blue lightning, his jaw clenched, his teeth bared like a puma about to spring.

"Wait, wait, mister," Raven said smoothly, despite the fear quaking in the pit of his stomach. "We have things to talk about."

180

"You'll talk no more." Sam said, holstering his six-gun.

"But don't you want to know what happened to the boy? You know I tried to save him from that Mexican . . ."

"You lying bastard," Sam said as Raven Dermott brought the rifle up with his toe and whirled on him.

Clubbing a glancing blow to Sam's head with the rifle, he ran for the chestnut. He caught the reins easily this time, and snapping a shot at Sam climbed into the saddle. Sam drew the Remington .44 and fired once, the bullet catching the big man in his right arm, breaking the bone.

The horse was spooked and on the run.

Sam's next bullet missed Dermott but burned a welt over the high haunch of the thoroughbred and set him off in a frenzied gallop.

Dermott lost the reins as his right arm hung useless.

All he could do was throw away the rifle, grab the saddle horn with his left hand, and hang on for dear life as the crazed horse, who could cover a mile in two minutes flat with the proper rider, made long leaping strides in the woods, dodging and weaving among the trees as Sam followed doggedly on foot.

The big horse had run less than fifty yards when he came upon the pitch-pine log with the upthrust snags that Dermott had used as his ambuscade.

The chestnut was trained to run, not jump. He was not an Irish hunter, and in a split second he balked, dropped his butt, and skidded toward the big old log with the pitch-pine horns angling out from its heart.

Raven Dermott hung on for dear life with his left hand, but his body was too heavy, and as the horse ducked and slid, he somersaulted out of the saddle and landed against the tree.

When Sam came hobbling forward, he saw a hook-ing pitch-pine snag protruding from Dermott's midsection and Dermott's body wiggling like a worm on a hook.

Dermott grabbed the pitch-pine limb with his left hand and tried to break it loose, but it was as hard as a bronze spear.

He tried to push off it with his feet and his left arm, but he was impaled through the guts, and the mad strength went out of him.

"Shoot me!" he screamed in agony as Sam came close.

"I'd rather set that log on fire," Sam said.

"Holy Mary, Mother of God, I can't stand anymore!" Raven Dermott screamed piteously. "Give me mercy at least."

"I'll give you about as much mercy as you give my Bobby," Sam said, holstering his six-gun.

"Don't leave me! I'm sorry!" Dermott coughed and whimpered, his face suffused with blood and covered with sweat, his eyes rolling in intolerable agony.

"I'll be back in a couple hours if I can find an ax. Likely you'll be chilled out by then," Sam said, turning to walk down the slope toward the house.

14

"This here mail's been chasin' you ever since you left Texas." The marshal's rasping voice was aimed at Thomas Lamb. Tossing a crumpled envelope adorned with foreign stamps over to the Englishman, Marshal Taylor addressed old Micah across the breakfast table. "Dermott had about fourteen thousand left in this leather poke with your brand on it."

"That'd be what's left of the herd money." old Micah nodded.

"I don't hold with overmuch bookkeeping." Frank Taylor shoved the bag across the table to the old man, who hefted it absently.

"Hardly seems worth all the killing, does it?"

"Criminals I've known never think about the punishment no matter how hard it's going to be," the marshal said. "Now, then, I thank you kindly for your hospitality and I'll be on my way to Austin."

As the marshal stood, so did Thomas Lamb, Sam Paterson with his left arm in a sling made from a dish towel, and Ruth, who wore a frilly apron over a simple gingham frock.

They shook hands all around, and Marshal Taylor stomped down the steps to his waiting horse. He tipped his peaked brown hat once after he'd mounted, then wheeled his sorrel gelding and rode down Paradise Valley, facing a thousand miles of a trail he knew too well already.

As Thomas opened the envelope and read the neat script carefully, Sam sat down at the table again with Micah. Ruth refilled his coffee cup and adjusted his sling, fussing around like a little dog in tall oats, until Sam laughed and said, "Ruthie, it isn't my birthday, is it?"

She stepped back, blushing. "No, Sam, I guess I never saw you hurt before. You was always such a big pine tree, I never could quite see the top of you."

"It'll heal." Sam smiled. "Then what'll you see?"

"You think I'd tell you!" She giggled and trotted out into the kitchen.

"I swear," Sam said, shaking his head.

Old Micah tried to hide the smile perking over his lined features. "She's luckier'n she knows. Both of you."

Sam colored and stared at his coffee cup. It was impossible for him to speak his mind about Ruthie. He just had to swallow what he wanted to say and hope she'd figure it out.

"It's from my betrothed," Thomas said into the silence, laying the letter aside. "She's not coming to America."

"That's too bad," Sam said. "I was looking forward to meeting her."

"It seems Oswaldine met a herpetologist chap . . ."

"A what?" Old Micah cocked his head in curiosity.

"A person who studies snakes. It seems it was love at first sight."

"Oh dear," Ruthie said, bringing in a platter of doughnuts. "You'll have to go back and win her all over again."

"I'm afraid winning is not the appropriate word." Thomas smiled. "And I don't think I'll try. Besides, they're already off somewhere catching the deadly venomous fer-de-lance, cobra, mamba, and krait."

"But why?" Ruth asked.

"Ah," Thomas said judiciously. "Because they're there."

"But she's your woman!" Ruthie said sharply.

"No longer." Thomas smiled sadly. "I daresay I must be content with my burdocks, purslanes, poke-weeds, and toothworts."

"You want to study the native plants, best go to the natives," old Micah said, a gleam in his eye. "Red Bird and his tribe, what's left of 'em, will be coming in to winter quarters soon. They'll set their tepees up at the lower end of the valley."

"I daresay no horticulturist has ever tried it."

"Somebody better before they're all gone," old Micah said. "Red Bird has a couple daughters that'd likely want to help in your studies."

"Indian girls?" Thomas blanched.

"They'd be cousins to Ruthie," Sam said quietly.

"Oh, what a clever fox you are, Mr. Campbell." Thomas chuckled.

"They've got to change and learn our ways," Old Micah said. "No matter if we're better or worse, it's got to happen, and you can help."

"A mission! You read me perfectly, Mr. Campbell." Thomas nodded jovially. "I'm not happy unless I'm saving something or growing something."

"They'll be back soon's the maple leaves turn color," old Micah said. "I'll speak for you."

"I noticed a few maple leaves going to gold this morning," Thomas said. "I daresay I'd like wintering in Paradise Valley."

"Just don't talk to 'em about God and hell and such, just talk about understanding and caring, and you'll do fine."

"Understanding the earth and its creatures and caring for them." Thomas nodded. "I'd have no trouble with that."

"I wonder what they'll name you," Ruthie said.

"Weed eater, likely," Sam drawled, and they burst out laughing.

Ruthie stopped suddenly and stared at Sam. "That was a joke!" she said, surprised.

"Anything wrong in that?" Sam asked.

"But I always thought you was such a gloomy stick!" she said, flabbergasted. "And you're jokin' most of the time, aren't you?"

"Likely you're finished learning." Sam shook his head solemnly.

"There you go. Now you're making fun of me because I'm so danged dumb!" she said angrily, her hands on her hips, leaning toward Sam.

"Anybody can make doughnuts so light they want to rise in the breeze can't be that dumb," Sam said, helping himself to another. "Likely you can bake a chokecherry pie, too."

"Likely," she drawled, imitating his deadpan manner.

"Reckon you got me." He grinned. "I can't go the game anymore."

"Why don't you two just spit it out that you want to make a team," old Micah growled. "Daggone it, you're making me nervous as a duck in the desert."

"Dad, it's not proper for you to ask. He's supposed to ask you. Isn't that right, Thomas?"

"I do believe that is the proper procedure." Thomas nodded judiciously.

"I ain't never been proper in my whole life and if I was, you wouldn't be here now," Micah growled. "Now quit this here do-si-do and speak your piece."

"I ain't got a ring," Sam said, scarlet-faced.

"You can use the one my Snow Bells wore. It belonged to my mother," old Micah Campbell said fiercely.

"Now just a minute, Dad . . ." Ruthie backed away, lifting the apron up over her face in mortification. "He's got to say it."

"We ain't got a preacher," Sam stammered.

"I daresay I could perform the ceremony if you care for the Anglican variety." Thomas smiled. "Entreat me not to leave thee, for whither thou goest, there I will go . . ."

"But—" Sam choked.

"See?" Ruthie dropped the apron. "See how he's looking for excuses all the time? He don't want me!" She started to cry, big tears welling out of her eyes.

"Ah, now, Ruthie," Sam said softly, standing and wrapping his good right arm about her, "don't back up on me, we're going to be all right."

"Then tell me flat out what you want," she demanded.

"I reckon I want you and me to ride together for about as long as forever is." Sam put his face in her blue-black crow's-wing hair and held her close.

"That's better," she said in a tiny voice.

Jack Curtis was born at Lincoln Center, Kansas. At an early age he came to live in Fresno, California. He served in the U.S. Navy during the Second World War, with duty in the Pacific theater. He began writing short stories after the war for the magazine market. Sam Peckinpah, later a film director, had also come from Fresno, and he enlisted Curtis in writing teleplays and story adaptations for *Dick Powell's Zane Grey Theater*. Sometimes Curtis shared credit for these teleplays with Peckinpah; sometimes he did not. Other work in the television industry followed with Curtis writing episodes for *The Rifleman*, *Have Gun, Will Travel*, Sam Peckinpah's *The Westerner*, *Rawhide*, *The Outlaws*, *Wagon Train*, *The Big Valley*, *The Virginian* and *Gunsmoke*. Curtis also contributed teleplays to non-Western series like *Dr. Kildare*, *Ben Casey* and *Four Star Theater*. He lives on a ranch in Big Sur, California, with his wife, LaVon. In recent years Jack Curtis published numerous books of poetry, wrote *Christmas in Calico* (1996) that was made into a television movie, and numerous Western novels, including *Lie, Eliza, Lie* (2002), *Pepper Tree Rider* (1994) and *No Mercy* (1995).